I0725430

Zero Tolerance

Elite Escorts 5

Lynn Burke

Copyright © 2023 by Lynn Burke

All rights reserved.

Editor: Kat McIntyre

Cover Artist / Photographer: Golden Czermak / FuriousFotog

Cover Model: Stephen Hughes

This is a work of fiction. Names, characters, places, and incidents are the product of the author's imagination or are used fictitiously, and any resemblance to actual persons, living or dead, business establishments, events, or locales is entirely coincidental.

No part of this book may be reproduced in any form, except for the inclusion of brief quotations in a review or article, without written permission from the author.

Visit my website at authorlynnburke.com

Zero Tolerance

As the owner of Elite Escorts, I have unlimited access to subs who crave domination without emotional ties. I never expected the business to make me a wealthy man.

But I'll be honest.

Seeing all my friends settle down has made me realize something is missing from my life.

My new secretary Jasmine is a librarian fantasy come to life. Her innocence calls to the sadist in me and every dark desire I have. But there's only one problem. She can't tolerate physical contact. Anywhere—at any time.

Psychological baggage from her childhood allows for friendship in the office but hinders a normal relationship. And the type I yearn for?

Hopeless.

However, when I offer myself to her to practice physical touch, I get a glimpse of what we could be.

But her past and present collide, threatening the fragile connection we've built.

Will the trust I've earned be enough to give her the courage to take another step forward? Or will submission to her wounds keep her from ever calling me Sir?

Prologue

Micah

Happy fucking eighteenth birthday to us.

Drunk off my ass, I grinned like a dork and inhaled the joint Dean had gifted me. My best buddy had hooked me up—both of us, really. We'd always been on the edge of kinky when it came to sex. Wanting to tie chicks up. Redden their asses a bit. Dominate in a way that would satisfy our mutual lust.

And Dean's weed supplier, Chaz? He knew a woman who was into that shit and wanted to give us both a taste of the lifestyle for our birthdays.

Dean drove since I was too damn wasted to even see straight. I tipped my head onto the headrest of his Tahoe's passenger's seat, New Hampshire's woods flying past my window in a blur. The radio cranked out some heavy metal shit he preferred. I didn't give a fuck about more in that moment than the burn in my lungs and the buzz in my blood.

Although we'd been born four days apart in states nowhere near each other, Dean and I headed north for our shared celebration. We were fresh out of high school, finally graduated, and about to become real men.

Well, we would be once we met up with Ginger—if that was even her real name.

Neither of us were virgins, but we'd never experienced anything outside of fumbling girls who didn't know their bodies any better than we claimed to. I'd made a few come, but that shit was hard work. An older woman seemed the way to go for a proper education, and I couldn't fucking wait to get my hands on her.

Getting higher by the second, I still sported a semi at the mere thought of finally marking up a woman's skin. Listening to her moan and beg for more pain with her pleasure. She wouldn't mind a little biting, probably. Nibbling, maybe?

Fuck, who was I kidding?

I wanted to sink my teeth into satiny flesh, leave indents behind. I lusted to see my ownership imprinted on her— handprints or flogger lashes. Wanted her quaking beneath me. Begging for my cock. Harder. Deeper.

"Fucking hell, would you hurry up?" I hollered over the ruckus Dean considered music while putting the joint out on the bottom of my sneaker.

He barked a laugh and turned down the radio a bit. "Can't wait to finally fuck an ass." A woohoo sound left his mouth as he pumped his fist out the open window. "Might even use my belt on her too. Chaz told me Ginger loves that shit."

"Pain, you mean?"

"Fuck yeah." Dean adjusted himself, glancing in the rearview before swerving into the right lane to exit off Route 16. "She's got a full-on dungeon in her basement.

Cross. Spanking bench. Hoist. Sex swing. And all the toys men like us dream about wielding."

That word *wielding* reminded me of swords and Thor's hammer, not exactly sexually charged images.

"Floggers and crops aren't weapons," I slurred, shaking my head and getting dizzy from the movement. "Whoa..." I snorted with laughter even though a deeper part of me worried about being high as fuck going into tonight. "The hell was in that joint, man?"

"The good shit." Dean winked at me and accelerated up a hill.

"Goddamn." I groaned and slumped into the seat, unable to keep my eyes open. Probably shouldn't have smoked the whole thing by myself.

"You gonna be able to pop a boner?"

"Shut the fuck up," I muttered, causing him to laugh again. "My dick will get hard when it needs to."

He would know. We'd shared girls a few times. The last being two girls home from college over winter break. Older, but not the types we fantasized about. I'd been high, drunk, and nervous that night, but when the time came to fuck, I'd risen to the occasion. And I'd been assured by the girl who'd let me smack her ass a couple times that I'd done a damn fine job of blowing her mind.

She'd tasted sweet as sugar...chocolate like the birthday cake Mom had made for me earlier in the day. A memory of blowing out the candles and my baby brother's tantrum over not getting any presents slid through my mind, but I had better shit to think on.

"What else do you know about this Ginger woman?" I asked Dean.

"She's thirty. A submissive who likes to play with

newbie Doms." He waggled his eyebrows. "*And,* she owes Chaz big time."

"What's she look like?"

"Who gives a fuck? As long as she's a warm, willing body with holes to fill, I don't give a shit if she's cross-eyed and missing teeth."

I grimaced, my standards a bit higher than my horndog friend.

Ginger proved to be easy on the eyes when she opened her front door to Dean's knock. Red hair hung around her shoulders, and her wide-spaced blue eyes were made up all smoky with liner and shadow. I lusted to see tear tracks lining her pale cheeks. Wanted her eyes watering while she choked on my dick while Dean fucked her ass.

She welcomed us in—at least I thought that was what she said. The rush of adrenaline only heightened the pulse thrumming in my ears, making it difficult to hear.

Too fucked up...

I ignored the voice in my head and followed on Dean's heels as Ginger led him through a kitchen...to her basement door. Somehow, I stumbled down the stairs without actually falling on top of my best friend.

"Welcome to my playroom, boys." It sounded like Ginger purred, but I wasn't really listening while taking in the dark red walls, one of which was covered with fun toys. Canes. Floggers. Paddles. Whips.

"Fuck," I groaned, my dick finally totally on board with what was about to go happen.

"Chaz told me you boys are new to the lifestyle."

Brand fucking *new,* I mused an echo for emphasis, blinking the St. Andrew's Cross in the room's corner into focus.

"Pay attention, dipshit." Dean elbowed me, turning my

gaze back toward him and Ginger. The images of them bled like wet paint...

I closed and rubbed my eyes. Fucking hell, I was fucked up. Bad.

Ginger...she was there to teach us shit—bondage and pain play she'd been into for over a decade. I needed to do what Dean said so I didn't miss out on a damn thing.

"I'm a switch," I heard her say, but Dean interrupted her.

"What's that?" he asked as a moment of clarity allowed the images of them to remain steady in front of me.

"It means I like to dominate or submit depending on my mood or needs." She glanced down over his frame, slightly smaller than mine. "Are you here to submit to me, or do you think you're man enough to take control and give me what I want?"

"I won't ever kneel for any woman," Dean declared, his chin raising a bit.

The back of him started to run like I peered at him through a rain-covered window. "But what if she begs for you to drop to your knees to eat her out?" I heard myself slur, the image coming to full-color life inside my mind. "I would definitely be down with that." Hell, my mouth watered for it.

Dean snorted but turned back toward Ginger. "How about you show me what you've got going on under that dress, pretty girl? Looks like nipple clamps. Got a plug up your ass too?"

I glanced over Ginger's tits, noting the bumps atop her nipples I'd missed before. Maybe they were simply pierced...

The colors of her smeared together, and I blinked her back into focus.

"Mmm," Ginger hummed. "Guess that answers that question. Good thing I'm in the mood for a spicy little boy like you."

"I'm not a *boy*," Dean shot back, his spine straightening—then wavering like a tear drop. "Guess I'm gonna have to prove it."

"Sounds good to me," Ginger agreed, dropping her dress to the floor, revealing her naked form. Dean had been right about the clamps, I noticed after another blink. They had sharp teeth. Bit into her pink nipples. Looked like they hurt.

He groaned and grabbed his bulge, starting for her.

Ginger held up her hand, halting him as her palm came into contact with his chest. "I'll let you top me, but first, I need to make sure you know the rules. My safeword for tonight is stop—to keep it simple."

Her voice was a buzz in my ears, and I couldn't seem to grasp what she'd said. I was too busy looking at those tasty buds of hers, wanting to rip off the clamps and sink my teeth into them instead.

Dean nodded. "Whatever you say, sweetheart."

"I don't do piss, shit, or spit. No degrading either. But feel free to give me whatever pain you can dish out. I like it rough."

"Fuck," Dean cursed. "That, I can definitely do. Micah too—if he can get the wool out of his ears and stroke his dick back to the weapon it is."

"Huh?" I knew Dean had addressed me, but had no fucking clue what he'd said.

Ginger walked to the spanking bench, her lush ass swaying with every step. "You wanna fuck, I'm game, but cover that shit up. My ass is yours too—but lube is a must. Got it?"

"Condoms. Lube," Dean muttered under his breath, ripping his clothes off.

*Condoms, lube...*his words repeated in my brain. Two of my own requirements. Not that I'd felt an ass wrapped around my dick yet. But I wouldn't ever hurt a woman intentionally by shoving into her without something to make it more comfortable. Didn't want to knock someone up at eighteen, either.

Dean's clothing dropped to the floor without any problems. There was no fucking way he was as messed up as me.

I struggled to take my boots off. Tripped while trying to rid my legs of my jeans. "Fucking hell, this is hard as shit," I said, suddenly cackling, not even sure I'd spoken aloud.

"Are you alright?" Ginger asked me from where she bent over the bench.

Was I okay?

Pretty sure that's what she'd asked, I nodded. "Had a little too much to drink for my birthday," I said, my words muffled by the T-shirt I tried to yank off overhead.

Ginger's gaze rested on my face once I managed to untangle myself. "Are you sober enough to give your consent to what's going down here tonight?"

I blinked her into focus. "Fuck, yeah," I stated firmly, stroking my semi in an attempt to wake the fucking thing up.

Her gaze dropped to my groin, and she licked her lips. She seemed on the verge of ordering me to shove it down her throat, but Dean stepped between us, cutting off my line of sight, which started to run along the edges again.

"Turn around," he said to her, his voice low. "Eyes on the floor. Widen your legs and show me your holes."

Shit. Swallowing hard, I stumbled around him to get a better view. I'd planned on letting Dean have first go at the woman, since he seemed to know more than I did about the BDSM lifestyle.

Ginger leaned over the bench as ordered, hands spreading her cheeks open. She'd waxed—or shaved—her pussy lips and puckered pink hole were void of any hair.

Or maybe I hallucinated and saw my fantasy.

"Jesus, she's pretty," I moaned, squeezing the base of my dick.

Dean slapped her pussy with his palm, hard enough Ginger jolted against the bench and moaned. "Like that?"

She muttered a curse, canting her hips higher. "Yes, Sir."

"Fuck yeah," Dean said, letting another palm fly. "Shit—you're wet. Look at this, Micah—her pussy is already dripping."

Did pussies actually drip? Arousal was more like... cream, not water. Right?

Fuck, my head...

I moved in close, standing by Dean's side as he shoved two fingers deep into Ginger's pussy. He groaned. Cursed. Fucked into her hole a few times. "Jesus, you're so damn hot for us."

"Hurt me, please," she begged, shifting on her bare feet.

Dean's gaze cast to the wall with all the toys. "What'll it be, sweet girl? Flogger? Paddle? Cane?"

"You're not experienced enough for a cane," Ginger said, her voice breathless.

A scowl dented Dean's forehead before it melted in front of my eyes.

I snickered.

He hated being told he couldn't do something. Hated when his dad's money couldn't get him whatever he wanted. I thought my baby brother at eight was a spoiled brat, but Dean was ten times worse than Sean ever was.

"Think I'll start with the flogger," Dean said, striding toward the wall—more like floating on water. "We'll take things from there."

Ginger talked Dean through his stance, how to hold the toy, and how to release lashes that would give the most impact, but I didn't hear a word. Barely could keep the two of them from liquifying into a puddle of color that sounded...golden? Maybe tinted with red?

I was hearing colors. Fucking lovely.

I snorted with laughter as Ginger claimed my best friend was a natural. A few lashes striped her skin a gorgeous shade of pink that reminded me of cotton candy.

My mouth watered.

Ginger moaned for more, liquifying into the bench. Or maybe I could no longer blink her into focus.

"Get me a paddle, Micah," Dean said, sending another slash of the flogger against Ginger's thighs.

I moved, my ears muffled, my blood seeming to churn sluggishly as I stood in front of the wall, unseeing. More numb than I'd wanted to be for Chaz's birthday present to us.

Goddamnit to fucking hell—I'd fucked up.

"Paddle!" Dean barked, making me blink into reality again.

I grabbed the closest toy off its peg and stumbled back to Dean.

My dick had deflated, I realized, glancing at his, which stuck straight up and leaked down its length. Or maybe his boner melted too. I snorted a laugh. "This shit turns you on," I heard myself say.

"It would turn you on too if you weren't so fucked up—shit, man," he whispered. "That's a cane."

"Huh?" I asked for clarity, not quite catching the words through his lowered tone.

Dean snagged the toy from me before I could process what he'd said and turned toward Ginger. "Tie her wrists up for me, Micah."

I blinked. She looked so pretty with her skin all flushed. Pussy glistening, thighs even wet from the arousal leaking from her.

Why wasn't my dick hard?

My best friend elbowed me. "Do what I said while she's floating there all sweet and quiet for us. Let's show her a real good time."

I found myself doing as Dean had instructed without conscious effort. Leather bindings were chained to the front of the bench, and Ginger didn't fight me as I clipped them in place around her wrists.

Dean had done the same to her heels, keeping her legs spread wide. "Suck his dick, sweet girl. Make him hard. I want his cum down your pretty throat when I unload in your ass."

Ginger opened her mouth, her eyes glazed over with lust.

I shuffled closer, holding the base of my flaccid dick to rub it over her lower lip.

She groaned and stuck out her tongue.

"Ah, fuck." I gulped as reality slammed into my brain, bringing me fully into the moment.

There was an older woman tied up in front of me, offering her mouth. A willing participant who'd given her consent for me to use her body to get off—that was all I cared about.

I slid my thickening length over her tongue, straight into her throat.

Ginger didn't gag, but tears welled in her eyes.

"Shit—so good," I slurred and cradled her face in my hands, backing out and pushing into her throat. "Fucking hell, Dean. Her mouth is heaven."

She jolted, shrieking around my dick.

Dean had hit her.

Sputtering, she tried to yank against her restraints.

I slid out, frowning. Blinking to keep her watering eyes from dissolving into liquid and sliding down her face. "Wha—"

Dean landed another blow.

Ginger yelped, her eyes becoming clear again. She twisted her head to look at Dean. Muttered something.

"Nuh uh. You *owe* him. Now, you gotta pay," Dean said, sweat beading on his forehead, his eyes glinting like I'd never seen before.

Maybe I was hallucinating.

I choked on a laugh. Yeah. Definitely was. Hearing shit too.

He stalked to a small table, grabbing something else from a basket while I tried to keep everything from shifting around me in a kaleidoscope of singing colors. Dick once more completely deflated and down for the count, I listened to my loud breaths weave through the harmonious tunes of blues and greens. Ginger attempted to get out of the restraints, but I couldn't make out the chains rattling. Or maybe they acted as the clanging cymbals in my ears.

She didn't look at me. Didn't make a demand.

I stumbled aside at Dean's shove, watching as he strapped a ball gag around Ginger's head. He squatted and held her chin while she writhed to escape his touch. "Be a good girl for me, Ginger, and I'll bring you so much pleasure you won't walk straight for a goddamn week." He slapped her cheek before rounding the bench.

"Let's count," he said, his tone jovial as fuck, laughter shadowing out the colorful music making my focus swim.

Shit.

I rubbed my eyes.

A red hand print blossomed on Ginger's cheek as she lifted her head to peer at me. Tears slid from her lashes, creating the dark makeup tracks over her skin that I'd hoped to see. She moaned, but I couldn't decipher her words.

Dean swatted her, once more sending Ginger lurching forward against the bench. She screamed around the ball gag.

"One!" he called, clear through the loud colors in my head. "After ten, I'll give you a break and fuck your ass. You'll be all squared up with Chaz. Deal?"

Ginger didn't answer. Couldn't since he swatted her again before she could utter a sound.

Sobs garbled around the ball gag, and Ginger's head drooped by the fourth, her body barely twitching with the next couple of hits.

"There's a good girl," Dean crooned. "Giving in to me. Your ass is on fire, babe. Gorgeous stripes from the cane."

The tune making my body sway went hazy—cut off abruptly.

Cane... I'd handed him...a fucking *cane?* I thought I'd grabbed a damn paddle off the wall.

My feet shuffled me around the bench, and I stared at the markings across Ginger's ass. One welt bled.

"Dean..." I muttered, shaking my head and almost toppling over from sudden dizziness.

"Shut up, Micah. She owes him—she consented to this."

"No—she didn't." At least, I thought she hadn't. Had she?

"Of course she did," Dean stepped back and swung the cane like a goddamned baseball bat. A welt rose immediately along the top of her thighs. Ginger didn't move.

"Is she okay?" I asked, not sure what was reality and what was fucked-up hallucinations.

"She's fucking fine." Dean hit her again and stepped back, heaving for breath and sweating. He shook, adrenaline definitely crashing through him. "Gotta have this ass." He smoothed a hand over her backside, in complete contrast to his violent lashings.

"Condoms, lube," I croaked out, remembering that much. At least, I thought I did.

"Yeah, yeah." Dean rubbed the head of his dick all over her asshole, then pussy, smearing pre-cum.

"Condoms," I repeated, but Dean fucked into Ginger's pussy, balls deep with one thrust.

"Fucking hell, she's wet. Shit. Never felt anything like it."

I blinked, trying to clear up my vision of the two of them morphing into one body. He wouldn't do anything she hadn't asked for...right?

I couldn't fucking remember.

Seconds blended into wavy minutes. Or maybe hours?

The image of Dean fucking Ginger into a single being undulated like one of those inflatable wacky waving tube men thingies...

What the *fuck* had been in that joint he'd given me? I rubbed at my eyes—stumbled away.

"Fuck, her asshole is strangling my dick," Dean groaned. "Sure you don't want a go?"

He'd taken her ass?

Condom, lube...he had neither.

My stomach clenched up tight, and I heaved, spilling sour beer and chocolate cake over the floor. Crawling, I attempted to escape the grunts ripping through my ringing ears. When had I fallen to my knees?

I lay my hot cheek on the cool floor. *I'm drunk.*

Fuck.

I rolled onto my back, my head spinning. Was I dying? Closing my eyes didn't stop the sounds of my best friend fucking Ginger's ass without the condoms and lube I swore she'd insisted on—but the darkness descending over my consciousness blocked everything out.

Chapter 1

Micah

Eighteen years later...

"I'm quitting."

I jerked my head up from the dark, hazy memories I'd dreamed about the night before. It had been years since that shit had haunted me.

Arms crossed, my secretary Dina propped herself against the doorjamb of my office.

"What?" I asked.

"I said that I'm quitting." Bland, expressionless hazel eyes peered at me, the same color as her sweatshirt.

"No fucking way."

"Fucking way." She smirked, and I thought again about how pretty she was, how lucky her fiancé was.

I tossed the file onto my desk and leaned back in my leather chair, narrowing my gaze. "You're giving me two weeks' notice?"

"Nope." Her smile widened. "You knew this was coming."

"I expected it with all that talk about needing time to plan your wedding and honeymooning for a month in Europe, yes, but what the fuck, Dina? On a Friday night?"

"

"This weekend is booked and all set. Everyone has their files, limos, and rooms are rented, goodie bags packed. Most of next week is all set too."

I heaved a deep breath, my lips pursed. Elite Escorts had been rolling along for over seven years and didn't show any signs of slowing. I'd hired a new escort a few days earlier, and the men and women employed by me were booked just about every weekend. Myself included. "And what am I supposed to do for office help? Payroll is Wednesday, for fuck's sake."

"I've got it covered, so don't get your panties in a twist. My baby sister is going to take my place."

"Just like that, huh?" I arched a brow.

"Yep. Just like that."

"Aren't even going to let me interview her first?"

Dina shrugged. "She's way more organized than I am, worked as a phone operator in sales, and is kind and honest. She'll fill my position without any issues. You'll probably be thanking me for quitting and bringing her in before the month ends."

"Awful confident," I muttered.

"Yep." She uncrossed her arms and straightened. "I'm bringing her here Monday and showing her the ropes, but she's on her own come Wednesday."

I grumbled a curse under my breath.

"I'm going out to grab some lunch, Mr. Grumpy Pants. Want anything?"

"You can stop at the liquor store and get me a bottle of Grey Goose for the shit you just dropped in my lap."

She chuckled and moved out of my sight into the reception area of the office addition I'd had included in the plans for my house Harper's Construction had just finished building. Dina left my door open. "Steak bomb?" she called, her keys clinking.

"Two!" I hollered back. "You owe me at least that! And, you can kiss your wedding present bonus goodbye!"

The shutting of the door cut off her laughter.

"Fuck." I scrubbed a hand over the clipped beard lining my jaw and glanced out the open window to watch Dina climb into her Saab in my driveway.

After getting caught staring at my first secretary's cleavage a few months into business and her crying foul, I'd been very careful about who I hired. While I had found Dina pretty the second she'd walked into my old office for an interview, there was no tug of want, no swelling of my cock at the thought of taking a flogger to her ass.

I hoped her sister would be the same.

A spring breeze rustled the file on my desk, and I put my mind back on the present rather than the past of last night's dream and the future with a new secretary.

Pulling my laptop closer, I considered the client lined up for me. At eight sharp, I would find Widow Mayfield bent over her late husband's desk. After our first session together, she'd gifted me a key to her swanky downtown Boston condo, promising to book me every other weekend.

That had been six months earlier.

I acted as her Dom, and she trusted me with her life, but there was no emotional pull between us. No deep connection binding us together.

She loved to have her ass reddened—hand, flogger, paddle—and anything I decided to use caused cum to pour from her pussy and pleadings from her lips. While she had hot, tight holes I enjoyed fucking, I'd grown bored with the arrangement. Thank Christ my cock at least was always up to the task, otherwise, I'd be popping blue pills like some of my employees when dick was on the menu.

I double-checked the schedule Dina had for the evening, making sure every I was dotted and T crossed. She hadn't ever screwed up, but I never took chances. Elite promised to please its customers, and once I gave my word, I never went back on it.

Ever.

Unfortunately, I'd learned the hard way what happened when mixing pleasure with inebriation. Lines blurred. Consent dissolved. Integrity broke apart and maimed innocent victims. My employees were allotted two glasses of alcohol while on "dates", and I personally vetted every person on my payroll. Background checks. References. Enough questions and blunt honesty about my expectations to even make the other Doms I'd hired squirm.

My intuition came from studying people because of poor judgment that had led to consequences which almost ruined my life.

Thank fuck for Dean's family name and the hush money his dad had dished out to keep us from going to jail. He'd shipped Dean back to the West Coast to live with his mom, and we had quickly lost touch.

For the best, all things considered.

With him gone from my life, I'd moved on from the mistakes we'd made. Learning how to become a real Dom, one who understood and honored the rules of the lifestyle, had been my focus. I'd proven to myself that such men existed, making it a point a few years earlier to clean up my guilt and shame over the entire affair.

And I'd built a business around the idea of ensuring pleasure could be found safely. I hoped like hell the bump in the road because of Dina leaving didn't slow the company down. Filling shoes, I'd learned, sucked ass. I'd recently lost an unofficial employee and three of my best escorts and had yet to replace the hole their quitting had created. It meant I'd personally taken on more of the physical workload, something I'd had no desire to do.

There was nothing wrong with getting paid to fuck—or act like eye candy—but I'd begun feeling empty after every evening I spent with clients. I wanted more.

Seeing Blake, Reid, Jarod, and Daniel start new lives with their so-called soulmates filled me with something I hadn't ever experienced before.

Jealousy.

I fucking hated it. Sure, I was happy as hell for my buddies, but our Sundays no longer consisted of guys, beer, good food, and sports. Christine came along with Jarod on occasion to hang out, but most times, I found myself alone or with my annoying little brother in my favorite threadbare recliner, me hollering at the flat screen while he trolled Grindr, looking for his next hookup.

"This fucking sucks," I muttered at my computer screen and pulled up my email, needing to bury myself in work.

JE

Widow Mayfield got the fuck of her life, coming around my cock four times while sweat dripped off my body. Preoccupation with the mess in my head had shut my balls down, but imagining my perfect woman, a demure outside the bedroom librarian-type creaming all over my cock, finally tipped the scales. I filled the condom, my fingertips bruising the widow's reddened ass cheeks.

She moaned beneath me, her pussy still trying to milk more cum from me, but I was so spent I wanted to topple over and sleep. I pulled out, and she whimpered. Smoothing a hand over her ass, I glanced up at her flushed face. Dark lashes fanned her cheeks. Perspiration dotted her brow.

"Be right back," I murmured, swiping the sweat from my own forehead.

My legs shook as I shuffled to the bathroom, and for the first time ever, I cursed my stamina and unrelenting brain. A quick cleanup and I wet a washcloth for the widow.

Aftercare was a must for all Elites regardless of how they pleasured clients, but it wasn't something Widow Mayfield had ever allowed. Independent and refusing to need a man ever again, she always insisted on looking after herself.

There were no soothing words or cuddling as she came down either.

It physically hurt for me to abstain from making sure she was okay. I handed her the towel, and she murmured her thanks, pushing up from where she'd sprawled over the antique oak desk.

"Feeling alright?" I asked, my hands fisted at my sides to keep from reaching for her.

"Mmm." She refused to look me in the eye, and I gathered my clothes. Less than two minutes later, I grabbed my keys off the file cabinet holding her late husband's sex toys.

"Thank you," she said, tugging on her red silk robe.

"My pleasure. Thank *you*." My fake-ass grin bothered the shit out of me, but I turned and left without another word—same as always.

It wasn't even ten, I,nd I headed to my empty lair, cursing my life. Money, a huge fucking house in Weston, a sweet, cherry-red '60 Ferrari...

I should have been happy as a pig in its own shit.

Should still be riding the high from pleasing a client and finding my own release.

Instead, emptiness like a black void ate at my mind, but I didn't have tolerance for depression. I refused to let it devour me like it had my father. He'd turned to liquor and had been battling liver issues for months because of his choice to wallow in the "woe is me."

I started my focus redirection by counting my blessings while exiting the highway. Thinking about all of my accomplishments—supporting my parents and paying Dad's medical bills. My sharp business mind and health. Youth. The mistakes I'd made that had instilled ethical values deep in my soul. The fact I didn't waste away behind bars for being an accomplice in assaulting that poor woman all those years ago.

"You've got it made, Fox," I muttered to myself while pulling into my long driveway, my headlights flashing through the trees and over the manicured lawn I paid big bucks to have installed and maintained.

But those things didn't erase the loneliness in my heart as my dark, silent home welcomed me without open arms.

Maybe finding a submissive woman to share it all with would fill the hollow feelings I couldn't seem to escape.

Chapter 2

Jasmine

Hands clenched on my lap, I peered out the windshield as Dina pulled into Micah Fox's driveway. "Holy shit, that's one hell of a house."

"Told you. Mr. Grumpy Pants has more money than that jerk-off sitting in the Oval Office."

A snort huffed from my lungs. "I doubt that."

"Seriously, though." Dina pulled to a stop and smiled. "He's a great guy. There's no need to be afraid."

I unclenched my hands and unclicked my seatbelt. "I'm not scared."

"Bullshit." She climbed out.

Grabbing my purse from between my feet, I followed suit, eyeing the stone monstrosity and all its windows in front of me.

"You'll have to shake his hand at least," Dina said while opening her car's back door and grabbing her bag, "but after that, you'll be all set."

"Did you tell him about...you know?" I asked, pulling my purse strap over my shoulder and smoothing a hand over the clingy material of my skirt.

Dina peered at me over the hood of her Saab as she slammed the door. "No, but I will if you want me to."

Lips pursed, I shook my head.

"Come on." She led me up the walkway to an addition on the right side of Mr. Fox's house and unlocked the door. A three-room area, she'd warned me in advance, a small space that filled quickly when the owner of Elite decided to work from behind his desk in the larger of the two offices.

Of the three days a week that I would act as Elite Escort's secretary, I would only have to deal with Dina's Mr. Grumpy Pants a couple of hours total. Most days, Dina had explained on the ride into Weston, he didn't even come to the office.

That was just fine by me. The less I had to interact with people in the flesh, the better life flowed for me.

"So, this is it." Dina tossed her purse onto a small table beside the door. "Bathroom is there—" she pointed to our right "—the door beside it leads to Mr. Fox's lair, and the one back there goes to his office. Like I said, tiny space."

I set my purse down beside hers and pulled the extra straight-backed chair from beside it behind the desk alongside hers. *Soon to be mine*, I reminded myself, glancing at an open door of Mr. Fox's empty office.

"He probably won't show until around lunchtime," Dina said, rolling her chair close to the desk. "Most Mondays he doesn't come in at all, but since I'm showing you the ropes today, I'm sure he'll swing in for a little while, at least."

I perched on the edge of the chair and clasped my hands on my lap again. My stomach twisted in knots, and I wondered if the breakfast Mom had made me would stay down.

"Want to take notes?" Dina asked, handing me a pen.

"Sure." My fingers shook, but I wrote down the voice-mail and email passwords as she logged in and showed me the daily tasks upon first arriving. I wrote precise details as she pulled up the files on a few of the escorts and explained how I was to go about forwarding their client folders to them as people booked with Elite.

By twelve, my stomach had settled, and I actually ate the lunch I'd packed. It took us two hours to get payroll done—two days early but dated correctly—since she wouldn't be in on Wednesday to walk me through the process.

A few phone calls came through, both of which she let go to voicemail for me to retrieve. She returned the first call —on speakerphone while I listened in to get a better feel for how she handled clients.

After a brief introductory discussion, Dina asked specifically what the woman was looking for.

A Dom. Someone to take control in a safe environment, flog or paddle her, and make her forget reality for a while. She didn't require penetration but wanted the option open if the mood struck.

I blinked, surprised by the woman's bluntness. While I knew Dina hooked up escorts with clients, I hadn't expected such...explicit sexual discussions. My palms sweated over the fact I had no personal experience whatsoever.

What the hell had I gotten myself into?

"We have a few escorts available that would fulfill your desires," Dina told her in a professional voice I'd never heard her use before. She was all smooth...like a sex phone worker might be.

I bit my inner lip. How the hell could I carry on that type of conversation over things I was clueless about? I wouldn't even know how to respond to the woman's request.

"I'll send over the paperwork in the next few minutes, and I'll also include direct links to some of Elite's best for you to choose from," Dina informed the new client.

A few minutes later, she hung up and glanced my way. "I probably should have talked to you about this before dragging your ass into taking over the job for me, but what do you know about the BDSM lifestyle?"

My expression probably clued her in to the thoughts clambering around in my brain, but I answered anyway. "Um...not a whole lot." I shrugged, my insides twisting again. I'd already quit my job—I needed this one. "I've read a few romance novels with stuff like bondage and spanking, but from what that client wants, it sounds like I've only peeked at the surface of a very deep rabbit hole."

"You have no idea," Dina muttered. She grabbed a notepad from the top drawer of the desk and jotted a few words down. "You get hyper-focused when wanting to learn something new, so I suggest you do that with this. You're going to need a crash course on all things BDSM. Learn what you can to better take these calls and make sure you know what you're talking about."

That I could definitely do since I had zero life outside of work and had nothing better to do.

She listed a few websites and even a forum I could join for free where I could ask questions from people who actually lived in what she wrote down as a D/s relationship, which she also explained to my clueless brain.

"There are a shit ton of other kinks," she said, handing me the paper. "A lot are listed on the limits form I'll be sending this new client."

I tucked the information into my purse with every

intention of memorizing the hell out of whatever BDSM entailed. A small part of me couldn't wait to get home to start since my interest had been piqued by the client's honesty about what got her off.

Dina clicked around on the computer a bit, showing me where all the pre-scheduling forms and contracts were located. She emailed the woman an NDA, client personal information sheets, payment agreement, the limits form, and a couple of other things for the woman to fill out. She included a contract example which Dina would complete when—if—the woman ended up choosing one of the Elites from the links she included in the body of the email.

"So how do you figure out who's a good match?" I asked, determined to not let Dina down and make this new job work for me.

Dina continued clacking on the keys while shrugging. "I've been at this almost from the beginning of EE. I know every single man and woman on payroll—and pretty well too. Micah does all the hiring, and the man is intuitive as fuck, let me tell you. The paperwork people go through, the physical, bi-monthly bloodwork, background checks...it's not an easy process."

"How many employees are into the BDSM thing?"

"We have a handful of Doms. Male, female, and one trans man. Here." Dina opened Elite's website and shifted her keyboard my way. "I gotta pee. Go ahead and browse a bit."

Nibbling on my inner lip, I glanced over the images and names of the men on hand to fulfill someone needing to escape reality with the inclusion of pain while sceneing. At least, I thought that was what Dina had called it while talking to the woman on the phone.

The second image snagged my attention, and I leaned forward to get a better look at the blond hottie.

Micah was his listed name.

As in Fox, the owner of Elite? Brow furrowed, I clicked on his profile and started to read his bio. He'd been a Dom and in the BDSM lifestyle for over fifteen years. His limits included scat play and water sports—I had no clue what either were. He was practiced in shibari. Again, I was clueless. I had more questions than understanding of what all he enjoyed dishing out to submissive clients wanting to slip into headspace, I think Dina had called it.

The toilet flushed, and I clicked out of Micah's profile. Two dark-haired men, a guy blonder than Micah, and an intimidating bald-headed guy were also on the main page of those available for the BDSM lifestyle.

"Find anything of interest?" Dina asked, heading toward her desk.

"Micah—is that the same Micah who owns EE?"

"Yeah. He's a Dom. Pretty good from what I've heard—our best, actually." She snorted while pulling her keyboard back in front of her. "Well, that's what he claims, anyway. The guy is an arrogant ass."

"I thought you said he was a decent guy."

"Oh, he is. He's just...confident and sometimes annoying as fuck. You'll see. Okay. So, moving on. Want to return the second call? The message said the man is looking for arm candy, not a fuck date."

I filled my lungs and slowly released it, nodding even though I'd rather climb beneath her—*my*—desk and hide. "Sure."

My hands and voice shook, but with Dina's help, I arranged for one of our female escorts to act as some rich man's date for a big charity event his ex-wife insisted he attend. He was a returning client and had already browsed the site to pick out his woman for the night, making the task a lot easier.

We scheduled with the man, then Dina showed me how to deal with the rest of the business. The limos and drivers, birthday cards to every employee, scheduling their bi-monthly testing, and putting the bills that came directly to the office on Micah's desk. He took care of all the finances except for ordering supplies for the escorts. Lube, condoms, and sex toys for the black bags taken along on any "date" outside of strict eye candy contracts came from one website she'd written down for me. When five rolled around—quitting time—my brain whirled, and Micah still hadn't come into the office.

"Guess you're waiting until Wednesday to meet him, Jaz," Dina said as she locked up behind us.

A warm breeze ruffled her long blonde hair, similar to my own. I'd pulled mine into a tight bun, hoping for a secretarial appearance, but it wouldn't have mattered if I'd left the skirt and low heels home in favor of the jeans and t-shirt Dina wore. At least I'd made an effort and would continue to do so to ensure I kept what seemed the perfect job for me and my issues.

But first—I needed to crash course myself in all things sex, kink, and otherwise.

Dina dropped me off at our parents with a good luck and sped toward her apartment she shared with her soon-to-be husband Aaron. Three months earlier, they'd moved in together, leaving me alone with Mom and Dad. The miserable middle child, Liz, had married young and had just given birth to her second son. He was an adorable little redhead with the softest cheeks and pouty lips I found myself able to snuggle and smooch without having a panic attack. Auntie loved when they came to visit.

I didn't mind being the only one still at home since I'd inherited Dina's much-larger room and her absence—along with Aaron's attachment to her side—meant one less person I might unexpectedly come into physical contact with.

My issues with physical touch had started years earlier, thanks to one of the many foster kids my parents had taken in, Billy. The bastard had issues of his own, sexual deviancies, which I ended up being on the receiving ass-end of. While the sicko hadn't taken my virginity, he'd done and said just about everything else possible.

It had taken me a long time to find the strength to approach my parents with the truth about what Billy had done, and he'd tried to slice my throat, exactly as he'd promised to do if I ever told anyone.

A shiver slid down my spine as I unlocked my parents' door and let myself inside.

He'd come after me a few years after being removed from my parents' home and being eighteen, ended up in jail for aggravated assault.

I ran a finger along the two-inch scar beneath my left ear, forcing myself to inhale normally. The memory of Billy's body odor, his bad breath, his cold, clammy hands on my skin...

My chest tightened as anxiety I was too well acquainted with began to run over my sensibilities.

Get a grip, Jasmine.

I counted my inhale through my nose and released it loudly through my mouth. In with the positive energy, out with the bad.

I am strong. I am able to overcome...

I chanted the various sayings one of my many therapists had suggested to talk down rising anxiety attacks.

"Is that you, Jasmine?" Mom's soothing voice floated down the hallway from the kitchen, helping to ground me.

"Yes," I managed to call back to her.

Dina had told our parents years earlier that Mr. Fox owned his own communications business. They never questioned her, and I wasn't about to tell them the truth about the sexual deviants I connected to fulfill fantasies and lust.

"How was it, sweetheart?" Mom appeared in the kitchen entryway with a crooked smile I'd inherited. I'd gotten her pale green eyes too, which had been called kind of creepy more than once.

"It went really well. I shouldn't have any problems settling in."

"Good." Her smile widened, and she motioned me back. "Hungry? I have a meatloaf in the oven and could use help peeling potatoes."

Meatloaf. I grimaced but nodded. "Sure. Let me just run upstairs and change first."

My new bedroom had been repainted from Dina's green to a soft cream. Long, shimmery blue curtains let in the sun, its rays falling across the new comforter from L.L. Bean I'd splurged on.

It was my safe haven, mine for as long as I needed, my parents had promised.

When Dina had decided she was done with work—her fiancé wanted her barefoot and preggo in the kitchen as soon as possible—she asked if I'd be interested in her position with Elite. No other employees in the office and only occasional visits with the owner even though the office was in his home?

Hell yes.

I'd jumped on the opportunity to only work three days a week and take home a bigger pay check than I'd been from making sales calls and getting hung up on ninety-nine percent of the time.

But I had a shit ton to digest—including knowledge about a lifestyle I needed serious schooling in. The last thing I needed was to sound like a fool when trying to match up clients for Elite. Learning would have to come after dinner though.

Meatloaf awaited.

I pulled on some yoga pants and a T-shirt before heading back down to help Mom finish with dinner. We'd always been close, and there wasn't anything I didn't share with her, but I shaded the truth about my boss and his company as she asked me about my day. Thank God for non-intrusive parents, because if their conservative asses knew I scheduled professional escorts and did up the boss's payroll for sex workers, they would probably blow a gasket.

Chapter 3

Micah

I opened the door to the office around one on Wednesday, mail in hand. The most luscious, sweet scent slammed into me, and I staggered to a halt two steps into the reception area. A quick glance around showed the room empty. I breathed deep, my cock twitching to life even though I'd jerked off in the shower an hour or so earlier.

Jasmine Swift, Dina's baby sister and my new secretary, smelled like...chocolate-covered strawberries. I prayed to God she wasn't anything to look at.

The flush of the toilet in the tiny bathroom sounded through the closed door, and I made my way into my office, tossing the mail on my desk. Rolling forward on my chair, I hit the power button on my laptop and glanced over the pile of direct deposits I needed to double check.

Payroll had at least gotten done. I wondered how Jasmine had settled in and if Dina had taught her everything she needed to know to keep my business rolling smoothly without too much of my intervention. So far, that road bump hadn't rearranged Elite's axel.

Please be an ugly troll...please God.

"Mr. Fox?"

Fuck. Husky and low, her voice shot straight to my cock. I lifted my head to find her standing in my doorway.

Blonde hair in a tight bun, pale-green eyes framed by dark lashes, plumped pink lips...fucking hell, the woman was stunning. I swallowed hard but couldn't help a quick glance down over the rest of her. She wore a button-up white blouse with a hint of cleavage peeking through and a pencil skirt hugging her hourglass figure.

Even without glasses, she was my librarian fantasy come to life, and my dick took notice hard and fast.

Clearing my throat, I smiled, hoping I didn't pass the fuck out with how quickly all the blood rushed from my brain to my groin. "You must be Jasmine."

She clasped her hands in front of her, her returned smile wobbling. "Yes."

I grabbed a manila envelope from the mail pile and stood, careful to keep my straining cock hidden behind it while striding forward to greet her. "Good to meet you," I said, holding out my free hand, needing to touch...feel her skin on mine.

Her lips parted, and she hesitated, gaze on my outstretched arm. "You, t-too." She slid her clammy palm against mine, and fuck me if pure lightning didn't shoot up my arm and straight to my balls.

I bit back a groan as she yanked her hand away as though burned by the same flash of whatever the fuck it was that had zapped through my body.

"Dina showed you everything you need to know?" My voice sounded strangled to my ears.

She wrung her hands together, her cheeks flushing and

chest starting to heave. "Y-Yes." Her eyes glazed, and she began to shake.

"Are you okay?" I asked, reaching out for her arm.

Jasmine stumbled backward in her heels and held up a finger as though asking for a minute. She spun and hurried to sit on the chair behind her desk, putting her head between her knees.

What the fuck? I furrowed my brow as I followed her, dick's excitement flagging from her strange behavior. "Jasmine?"

She held up the same damn finger while attempting to suck down oxygen.

"Asthma?" I asked.

"P-Panic attack," she gasped out.

My brow shot up. From simply shaking my hand? I knew I had a Midas touch, but goddamn. My ego swelled, but her lowered head and shuddering frame furrowed my brow deeper. I squatted in front of her, taking care to give the woman some distance even though my fingers itched to reach out and comfort her. "Breathe with me, Jasmine."

Counting, I led her through some lung exercises as I'd done before with subs when they became overcome by anxiety. Her sweet scent flooded through me, and I fought to keep from leaning closer to inhale her exhales.

At least the awkward situation made my dick completely limp, regardless of her close proximity.

"Okay?" I asked, checking in with her after a few minutes.

"Hmm." She lifted her torso and sat back in her chair, eyes still closed. "Sorry."

"No need to apologize." I had no fucking clue why she had.

"I left the payroll on your desk to look over," she said, her words rushed and breathy.

"Are you okay?" I asked again, making sure she was before grilling her for why she'd reacted to me in such a way.

"Being an Elite pays ten times better than any job I've had before," she rushed on, ignoring my concern, her hands fluttering from one thing to another on the desk. "I'd join the team in a heartbeat if I didn't have these damn contact issues."

"Huh?"

Her face reddened. "I...um, shit. I-I didn't mean to... well. Fine." She huffed. "I don't like to be touched."

"When?"

"Ever." She finally turned her gaze toward me.

Lust shot through me again at her clear vulnerability. Embarrassment. Innocence.

So. Fucking. Fucked.

"Shaking my hand caused that attack?" I asked quietly, trying to not give off imposing vibes like I'd been told I tended to do.

Jasmine nodded. "I react the same way anytime someone other than my sisters, Mom, or my nephews comes into contact with me." Shaky laughter jostled her breasts, and I fought not to lower my attention below her nose. "You should have seen me at my doctor checkup last month. It was hellish, and that was with a Xanax in my system." Another bout of nervous laughter escaped her lips.

I stood and stepped back, allowing her the personal space she would need—fucking always. "Shit. That must really suck."

Jasmine shrugged but didn't quite pull off acting nonchalant. "I'm used to it, but yeah. My issues have kept me from experiencing a lot of things in life." Pink flushed her face in the same way I expected arousal would do.

I scrubbed a hand over my scuff as a low chuckle huffed through my nose. I wanted to ask if she'd ever gotten laid. When she'd last gone out with a guy. Ever been kissed? Held hands?

Talk about a goddamn diamond in the rough. To have such an innocent woman—

Control, Fox. Goddamnit all to hell.

The woman didn't like to be touched for fuck's sake.

I tried for a smile, attempting to get a hold on myself I didn't usually struggle with. "Well, I promise to keep my hands to myself at all times."

A hint of a frown furrowed her brow for a split second, but she smiled, gazing up at me with clear green eyes I could easily drown in. Lose myself.

Fucking witchery.

"Dina told me you're a man of your word," Jasmine stated quietly.

I couldn't help my grin. "She also calls me Mr. Grumpy Pants, but yes, I am. If I make a promise, I keep it. No matter what."

She blew a heavy exhale between her plump, parted lips I could *not* stare at. "Thank you for understanding."

"Not a problem." I turned back toward my office but paused in the doorway. "Glad to have you here, Jasmine," I said, glancing at her one last time.

Her smile widened, and her body slouched in the chair as though relieved I didn't seem to give a shit about her... issue. "It's good to be here, sir."

Fuuuuck.

A groan rose in my chest at her choice of title. No way

in hell she would say that to me knowing what it meant. "Call me Micah," I croaked. "Please."

"Okay. Micah."

"If you have any questions, please don't hesitate to ask." I shut my office door and slumped on my chair. Why hadn't Dina warned me about her sister? I hated to hurt anyone unless we were under agreement and sceneing together. Given a green light, I never held back dishing out whatever would offer a willing participant release.

Jasmine Swift might appear a timid, shy submissive, but she was off-limits, way beyond the fact that she worked for me.

I scrubbed a hand along my clipped beard again and whispered every curse word I knew. How the fuck was I supposed to work with a woman like that all up in my space three days a week? Her perfume alone made me want to grab my cock and empty my balls. Those lips, those tits, a perfect landing place for my cum. Those hips and that ass...

Jesus fucking Christ, I was in trouble.

"You're a master of control, you horny bastard," I muttered to myself, all the while stroking myself through my jeans. "Either go fire her right now or plan on jerking off a couple times a day, three days a week."

If she wasn't Dina's baby sister I'd have sent her packing without a second thought.

I glanced up at my office door I'd intentionally closed, straining for noises she might make. A drawer opened. Keys on the computer clicked. An image of her on her knees peering up at me with those big green eyes rose out of nowhere, and I did groan.

Time for another fucking cold shower—or at least putting some distance between us.

Chapter 4

Jasmine

Micah announced he had to leave not long after shutting himself in his office. Heat flushed my face, and I couldn't meet his eyes when he came back out to the reception area, cleared his throat, and said he had some stuff to take care of.

I'd watched his shoes in my periphery until he started toward the door leading outside. I turned and enjoyed an eyeful of fine man eye candy. His sandy-blond hair faded in the back but was longer and mussed on top, same as the image of the Micah listed as one of Elite's Doms. Broad shoulders, narrow waist, and long legs, thick thighs hugged by jeans... *How a man's jeans ought to fit,* I thought as drool flooded my mouth.

My boss took care of clients who needed a little pain with their pleasure, and I wondered if he got off on it too or just fulfilled his role to pay for that second home he had down in Cancun Dina had told me about.

I'd stayed up way too late the night before checking out the first website she had written down for me, falling down a hole deeper than any rabbit's. Images had struck me—

burned into my memory. I'd even watched a GIF that show-cased a woman strapped to a bench getting her ass whacked with what looked like a paddle. I may have stared as it replayed a few too many times.

My ass had clenched in an...arousing way, and I'd shut my laptop down, telling myself I'd had enough for one night of schooling.

But I couldn't wait to dive back in later that night and learn some more. My blood actually heated at the thought of maybe someday being "normal" and able to handle a man's touch. Would I like some pain with *my* pleasure? From my body's reaction to the GIF, I wondered a little too hard, fantasizing about that very thing.

Micah's red sports car disappeared down the driveway, and I sighed, sounding like a lovesick schoolgirl. I hoped he would stop in before I left for the day, but no such luck.

I locked up the office a few hours later and dialed Dina while walking to my car. "Hey," I said before she finished saying hello.

"How'd it go?"

"My God, Micah is damn hotter in person than his profile pic on Elite's website!" I whispered while climbing into my car. "Why the hell didn't you warn me he was so damn swoon worthy?"

"Are you okay?" Dina asked, sounding preoccupied.

"Yes." A smile and sigh shuddered through me as I started the car and blasted the AC. "He's the first guy I've actually wanted to touch me since, well, you know."

"Did he?" she snapped, and I imagined my big sister had stilled, ignoring whatever had required all her attention seconds earlier.

"We shook hands. Briefly. I actually did it by choice!" Nervous laughter bubbled again at the memory of his skin sliding against my palm. "I pulled away before he finished squeezing, and he actually helped me down from the resulting panic attack. He was so sweet. Makes me want to try again."

"He's not right for you."

My smile faded as I pulled my seatbelt across my chest and buckled myself in. "Why ever not? He was very concerned for me and behaved like a perfect gentleman—"

"He's slept with hundreds of women."

"So what? I *actually wanted a man to touch me.*" I emphasized my words, reminding her of what that meant for me. "That's a major step in recovery! Even better, I'm thinking about doing it again!"

"Well, your therapist wouldn't recommend you get involved with a man whore."

"Oh, my God, Dina." I shook my head and stared at Micah's locked office door directly in front of me. "I took a single step forward, and you think I'm just going to bend over and let him have his way with me?" A shocking pulse rippled through my core at the image crashing into my imagination.

Her snort of laughter held no hint of amusement, and nothing about my body's response to the image in my mind was funny. It was warm. Addictive.

"If any man could talk you into it, Micah Fox is the one," Dina muttered.

I remembered the concern in his eyes and the sincerity in his tone of voice while counting and breathing with me. "He promised he wouldn't ever touch me again."

She didn't reply.

Yeah, I thought, putting my car into reverse. *That shut you right up.* "You said he's a man of his word."

"He is."

"All right, then. No need for you to worry."

She sighed loudly in my ear, and I could see her lips pursing just like Mom's. "Just be careful, Jaz."

"I'm always am."

I hung up a few seconds later and pulled out of his driveway. The giddiness I'd felt earlier over coming into physical contact with Micah and not going full-blown into panic mode refused to diminish regardless of my Debbie Downer of a sister.

My laptop waited for me at home.

I couldn't wait to dive deeper into the world my boss preferred to live in.

JE

I lay in bed that night after spending about two hours too long staring wide-eyed at my computer screen. A notebook and pen lay on my bedside table, page upon page covered with notes. Power play. Consent. Safewords. Aftercare. Different types of bondage. Suspension. Daddies and littles. Masters and slaves. Punishment and sensory play.

All included physical touch in some way, shape, or form.

Micah came to mind for like the hundredth time that day since I first saw him sitting at his desk. Behind my closed eyelids, his damn hair stuck up, making my fingers itch to rearrange it. A short, groomed beard lined his square jaw I wanted to pepper with kisses. He had a perfectly shaped nose most male models would die for. Those blue eyes of his had darkened as he'd enjoyed a once-over down my body like he'd done when taking note of my presence in his office doorway.

Although quick, his gaze had seared my skin beneath

my clothing, and I'd felt arousal like never before, unlike any steamy scene in a romance novel brought to life between my thighs.

Yes, I'd wanted his touch and not just clasping my hand in greeting.

I had tossed out "sir", but I hadn't known at the time what that word meant to him if it'd been with a capital S. Perhaps that explained the stiffening of his back when I'd addressed him as such. I would need to stick to his first name as suggested.

A fantasy filled my mind, one where I called him Sir. Could stomach his touch—enjoyed it, even. Nipple clamps came first, the metal teeth biting into my flesh like they had done with a woman I'd watched on video earlier that night. Like her, I would have a vibrator run over my pubis, down to my sopping pussy and back up to my throbbing clit.

I bit on the inside of my lip as I danced my fingers over myself, imagining it was Micah's hand. His flesh caressing mine, tongue lapping at my wetness as the Dom in the video had done with his sub. Nibbling along my swollen labia with just a hint of teeth to sting...

I sprang ahead in my mind toward the good stuff.

A hungry kiss, Micah's sweet breath flooding my senses as he thrust his cock into me, finally taking the V-card I never expected to be rid of.

"God," I groaned, writhing beneath the onslaught of my own searching touch. I couldn't reach deep enough into my needy body. Wasn't full enough with the two fingers I managed to push into my tightness.

I flicked my clit with my free hand, pinched, and rubbed until my climax tingled to life and crested, my pussy pulling on my fingers as cum leaked from me. Heaving for breath, I finally stilled, my pulse thrumming in my ears.

I'd never come so hard in my life.

I couldn't begin to imagine what the real thing would feel like, but holy hell, did I want to find out.

Micah had told me I could go to him any questions I had. I wondered if asking how certain sexual fantasies played out counted as a topic of appropriate conversation.

Chapter 5

Micah

I climbed out of the shower, my adrenaline still racing from emptying my balls to thoughts of Jasmine's lips wrapped around my cock. Telling myself I needed to keep my distance and stay away from the office for a while, I toweled off.

My phone dinged, and I grabbed it from the bathroom counter.

Dina: **If you do or say anything inappropriate to my baby sister, remember that I know ALL of your secrets. Elite is worth more than another notch on your goddamn bedpost, Mr. Fox.**

Chuckling, I texted back with three thumbs-up.

She replied with an evil devil face.

A few minutes later, I poured more coffee, and the phone rang. "I got the message loud and clear, Dina," I said in answer before she could speak.

"I was going to text you again, but it was too much."

"What's up?"

Dina huffed a sigh. "You're the first person Jasmine has ever *wanted* to touch her."

My brow shot up, and the hand lifting my coffee to my lips paused. I considered a sexual comeback but bit my tongue.

Jesus fucking Christ.

"I can imagine what you're thinking, which is why I called rather than texted," Dina said when I didn't comment. "Her desiring physical contact with a person is a huge step in recovery from her trauma."

"Trauma? Is that what caused her contact issue thing?" I sipped my coffee.

"Did she tell you about it?"

I settled on a stool at the island. "No, just that she doesn't like to come into direct contact with people outside of you and Liz, your mom, and her nephews."

"Well, it's not my story to tell."

While I wanted to ask a million questions and get to the bottom of what held Jasmine back from experiencing intimacy, I wouldn't pry into people's personal shit. Fuck knew I couldn't stand when people asked about my past either. "Fair enough."

"Anyway, if you could just be her friend and maybe slowly introduce her to more appropriate, friend-like physical touch, I would forever be indebted."

"Are you asking this so I'll still give you that wedding bonus I'd promised?"

She laughed, and I sipped my coffee again. "No. I'm asking because I love my sister and hope for her happiness more than anything." Her exhale sounded loud in my ear. "And, I trust you. Otherwise, I never would have allowed Jaz to work for you."

A pleasant tingle warmed my chest, but I grinned. "So you're saying you want to hire me to pleasure your sister?"

"Ha! As if."

"I'll do the friend-zone touching if she's up for it for free because I adore you."

"You're a pretty cool cat too, Micah."

Fifteen minutes later and still grinning, I headed into the office rather than taking off for the day like I'd intended to do in order to avoid Dina's baby sister. I kept glancing at the clock, fidgeting while waiting for Jasmine's arrival rather than getting some work done.

A car engine sounded outside in the driveway, and a strange twinge lightened my chest. Minutes later, the outside door opened.

The scent of chocolate-covered strawberries swept into my office on the cross breeze from my open window allowing in the spring's warmth. I filled my lungs, my mouth watering and cock swelling. "Jasmine?" I called a few minutes later, having given her time to settle in.

She appeared in the doorway in a similar button-down and skirt as on Wednesday, her hair pulled back in that damn bun I wanted to unravel and watch as a blonde waterfall fell over her bare shoulders.

I held up a file as my dick swelled. "Medical forms and signatures for the two new clients this weekend. They'll need to be scanned and uploaded to the system."

She moved across the room and took the file from me, keeping her hand on the opposite end. "I'll do it right away."

"Also—" I pulled in closer to my desk to hide what she did to me "—see if Anthony is available to fill in with Mrs. Mayfield next Friday night. If so, contact her and ask if the switch will be okay."

I blinked at my unplanned order, wondering where the fuck it had that come from.

"Sure thing."

I nodded, and she left, her fine backside drawing and holding my gaze. I lusted to sink balls deep inside of her—pussy, ass—whatever and whenever she allowed.

Fuck. Another hand scrub along my jaw prickled my palm with too-long whiskers. Temptation to fire her just so I could pursue her toyed in my brain, but I'd made a promise to Dina. I'd also told Jasmine I wouldn't touch her since she *didn't* want anyone's hands on her.

I had no choice but to simply be her friend. Set her at ease and get to know her. Eventually, she might realize that I was no threat. Maybe at some point, she would be open to the casual friend-like touching Dina hoped might happen between the two of us.

It was going to be a long fucking day since all I could hinge on was hope—and I couldn't stop thinking about how smooth her skin felt on my fingertips. What she tasted like on my tongue—

"Control, Fox," I muttered at myself. "The fuck is wrong with you?"

Jasmine.

But she was also so goddamned right my balls ached.

ℲF

Sunday—man cave, sports day arrived. I'd sent out the text for my buddies to swing by, but Cooney was the only one available. He brought fresh-baked chocolate chip cookies from Becky, and I chowed until my stomach turned cankerous.

I groaned and settled back in my old recliner I refused to replace. "That woman of yours sure knows how to bake."

"Goddamn right." Cooney patted his abs, his deep voice grumbling.

I chuckled and sipped my beer but set it aside when I realized I wasn't going to fit anything else down my esophagus. "Are you honestly happier having her in your life?" I asked even though his face betrayed him when he'd used to be a stoic, closed book.

"Fuck yes. She's the best thing that's ever happened to me."

A twist of jealousy tried to make its way through my gut. I thought of Blake, Reid and Jarod, all of whom had left Elite after losing their hearts. Reid had inherited a little girl when he'd hooked up with Jessica, and they also had a baby of their own. Jarod and Christine hung on each other every time I saw them. They all used to sicken me, but the mental image of Jasmine clinging to me like that definitely changed my mind.

My cock twitched, but it was the thought of the trust she would be showing with that kind of action that appealed to me most. Imagining the D/s relationship we could have if I helped her heal from whatever wounds scared her filled me with a desire I'd never experienced before.

I cleared my throat. "So I've got this problem."

"Yeah?"

"My new secretary is hot as fuck, and I don't want to keep my hands to myself."

Cooney chuckled and shifted on the couch, stretching his legs out on the ottoman. "You've got a problem alright."

"It's Dina's sister—"

"Oh, shit."

"—and she doesn't like to be touched."

"Sounds like the poor little rich boy can't have what he wants for a change," Cooney mocked.

I tossed a pillow at his head which he easily ducked and avoided. "Dina asked me to be her friend. Help her conquer her issues since I'm the first person Jasmine has actually wanted to touch her."

"So it's not that she isn't interested in physical interaction."

"Right." I moved around on my chair, trying to get comfortable. Damn cookies. "I'm really not liking Becky right now."

Cooney chuckled. "What happened to your usual self-control?"

"Out the fucking door," I muttered, uneasy in a whole different way. I didn't do shit on a whim. Spontaneity and I didn't coexist in the same reality thanks to that night Dean and I had driven into New Hampshire and about ruined our lives.

Unaware of my past, Cooney continued laughing, and I watched my friend's dark eyes twinkle with happiness. Becky had given him too much joy to keep contained.

Lucky bastard.

"So what caused Jasmine's issues?" he asked.

"Not sure. Isn't really something I can just ask about."

"Dina said you're the first guy her sister has actually wanted physical contact with?"

My cock tried to twitch again, but my stomach hurt too fucking much to pay it any mind. "We shook hands, and she started to have a panic attack, but yeah, guess she told Dina something different from what I expected after I helped her get ahold of her breathing."

"You gonna be able to help her without losing control like you did with the cookies?"

"Fucking prick," I mumbled.

He laughed, then groaned, holding his stomach. "Honest question."

I huffed a breath. "If I jerk off a dozen times a day, maybe I can keep from doing something stupid."

"You could always fire her," Cooney said a few seconds later. "Out of sight, out of mind."

I considered his words for a few minutes, same as I'd done that first time I'd laid eyes on her. "I'm in too fucking deep already." Silence settled, and I glanced over at my buddy to find him peering at me, a grin on his face. "The fuck is on your mind, Cooney?"

"You're crushing like a high schooler."

Turning away, I closed my eyes and rested my head on the back of the recliner. "Fuck."

He laughed again, deepening my scowl. "You gonna quit Elite too?"

I snorted, pretending I hadn't already thought long and hard about taking my name off the list of available Doms for hire. "Fuck no."

"Get involved with her, and she'll definitely want you to stop being an escort. No woman I've ever met likes to share."

"Oh, I've met quite a few of those," I stated, having dated a bit before giving up the drama for emotionless trans-actions that earned me money. "Never even considered putting aside my free lifestyle, but if Jasmine's insides match the beauty of her outside?" I shrugged, my groin on board with what I might have already set my mind on.

"Holy shit. Never thought you'd ever consider an exclusive relationship."

"Yeah, well, shit happens," I said with a shrug, knowing in that moment that I *did* want Jasmine. From what I'd seen and heard from Dina over the years, her youngest sister was one hell of a woman and would make a great partner in life.

His deep chuckle caused my grin to widen, and I ignored the Sox game and focused on finding a way to make her mine—and comfortable with my hands on her body.

Chapter 6

Jasmine

On Monday, Micah was sweet as blueberry pie, putting me at ease before the first hour passed.

"I'm going to make coffee," he said, coming out of his office. "Want a cup?"

I smiled up at him but quickly looked away. His intense blue eyes caused my stomach to flutter and my fingers tingle to touch the scruff along his jaw. "Sure."

He headed for the door leading into his house, and I enjoyed another eyeful of his fine backside before he disappeared from sight.

Sighing, I turned back to my computer screen and the order I'd been putting together on the sex toy website Micah purchased supplies from. My attraction for my boss was troubling enough, never mind having to look at kinky items that got my mind going.

Butt plugs...

Teeth holding onto my lower lip, I scrolled down through the various shapes and sizes. They were something that definitely interested me. Dildos too. Vibrators. Cuffs, crops, and floggers. I'd seen them all on various websites over the weekend while "studying".

I'd also stumbled across a free porn site, and while I expected the scenes played out in front of cameras contained a bit of theatrics for those getting off on watching, I had somewhat of a handle on what it meant to be a submissive in Micah's world.

Even better had been a personal blog from a woman living the lifestyle with her husband for over twenty years. Talk about swoon-worthy and the happily-ever-after I craved for myself.

Dampness coated my panties, and I squirmed on my chair while browsing through the website's toys. Thick wooden paddles. Obscene dildos shaped like a dragon cock. Butt plugs with enough girth my asshole clenched.

A cane caught my eye. While I wasn't sure I would enjoy the type of severe pain I'd read came with that particular item, my body seemed interested in finding out. Nipple clamps, though? Yes, please. I'd found pinching rather than flicking my tight nubs when masturbating over the weekend had sent me rushing over the edge ten times faster than a passive caress.

A shiver slid up my back, and I turned.

Micah stood in the open doorway to his private lair. His gaze flitted from the computer screen to my face.

Warmth rushed through me at the heat in his eyes, and I jerked back toward the computer, minimizing the website window displaying various clamps with sharp-looking teeth. "I'm just placing an order." The words rushed from my mouth. "I wasn't sure if you wanted me to get the same old, same old, or if we should try out some new items."

I'd said we.

Oh, God! My face flooded with heat. "They. You. I-I

mean the escorts." My forced smile wobbled. "With clients."

Swallowing, I peeked at him, and my smile faded.

One eyebrow cocked, he smirked down at me, but that heat still simmered in his eyes. "You have permission to order whatever you desire, Jasmine."

"Th-thank you, sir."

Shit!

"Micah. Thank you, *Micah*," I corrected myself.

Chuckling, he disappeared into his house again. I buried my face in my hands, my stomach in knots and my skin sizzling from head to toe. What did he think of me? Had he seen me squirming on my chair to ease the twinging between my legs?

"Oh, God," I muttered into my palms.

"Jasmine."

I jolted upright, face even hotter.

Micah handed me a cup of coffee, eyes twinkling, his lips still curved upward.

"Th-thanks." I stared—considered brushing my fingertips across his—and glanced up again into his eyes.

He spun the mug so the handle faced me. "Here."

I accepted the coffee without touching him and slumped back in my chair. *Should have gone for it*, I told myself while sipping. The thought didn't stir anxiety. Only longing.

Rather than walking into his office, he lounged on the chair across from my desk.

Flutters of something stirred in my belly, and I smiled for real. "Thanks for the coffee."

"You're welcome. So." He stretched out his long legs. "What toys would you want in those magic bags we send along with our escorts if *you* booked someone for the night?"

Another rush of warmth swept through me, flaming my face and making me squirm in my seat again. "Uh..."

"I'm asking for professional reasons, as your boss, not to appease my own kinks."

Oh, God.

"Okay." I cleared my throat but couldn't make myself look at him to see if his eyes betrayed a lie. Dina had said he was trustworthy—and I believed my sister. "I think you've got the basics covered already, and we add additional items by request, right?"

"Yes."

I shrugged and pulled the website back up onscreen. "N-Nothing, then, really."

"What about the nipple clamps you were checking out? Their teeth appeared a little more hardcore than the ones we currently have."

Curses rang between my ears at Micah's suggestion. I couldn't look at him. "Um...sure?"

"Maybe we should have a dragon cock dildo in stock in case a client is feeling extra brave. Or, at least bigger sized plugs."

He sipped his coffee while I attempted to keep from choking on my own saliva. How long had he been watching me?

"Paddles with holes leave beautiful patterns on the skin," he continued, his voice hinting at a sensual smirk, "but canes are my absolute favorite."

My lungs constricted but not from panic. Why did my boss have to speak about things that stole my breath in a good way? I wanted to moan. Curse him for being so damn hot. The thought of going out with Micah and having one of those bags at his disposal made the walls of my pussy pulse, and I slammed my eyelids shut and squeezed my thighs together.

Breathe, Jasmine...

"If you could go any place in the world, where would it be?"

His off-the-wall question snapped me back to the office, slamming the car I rode toward arousal to a halt. "Huh?"

"Bucket-list vacation—where would you go?" Zero heat lit his gaze, and his smirk lifted into a full, friendly smile rather than the suggestive one I could have sworn he'd worn seconds earlier.

"P-Paris," I shared where I'd always dreamed of traveling.

"Why Paris?"

"It seems like the place for lovers."

"Who would you take along with you?" He swigged his coffee, gaze still on me.

I opened my mouth but shut it again and shrugged.

"No boyfriend?"

"No."

"Sorry." He cleared his throat and glanced out the open window. "That was a shitty question to ask, considering..."

"It's okay," I said even though the reminder slammed the stark truth back into my fanciful head. "I've never had a boyfriend. Never even kissed a guy."

"Shit," he muttered and shifted on the chair.

"Yeah. It sucks." My attempted smile wobbled again. "I-I think I'm on a new road to recovery, though."

His focus settled on my face again. "Why's that?"

"Because I found I'm actually comfortable around someone else—*you*. For the most part, anyway."

He grinned. "Glad to hear it."

"Yeah." My own smile widened. "Not sure why, but I

don't get all freaked out when you get close to me." Not in a bad way, at least. For some reason, I *liked* being near him. He made me feel...safe. Even though I hardly knew him, I was sure I could tell Micah anything and he wouldn't scoff or laugh. Dina trusted him too, which definitely held weight in my opinion.

"Would it be inappropriate if I offered my help?" he asked. "I mean, if you're up for testing yourself...like if you ever wanted to shake my hand again to see how you would react, I'm available."

This man.

"Thank you," I whispered, sudden tears pricking my eyelids.

He pushed up from the chair and lifted his coffee my way in cheers before heading into his office.

I stared at my computer screen, unable to see through the tears making the images waver before me. Falling for him would be so easy—*too* easy.

※

I settled into the routine of being Elite's secretary, and the silly flutterings whenever Micah came into the office calmed down a bit. He stopped in every day I was on the clock, much longer than Dina had told me before I'd taken the job.

At least once a week, we locked up the office for an hour or so and went out for lunch. Subs, pizza, salads—nothing fancy or indulgent that I considered a date. We discussed business rather than personal things like a couple getting to know one another would do, and I eventually lost a bit of my shyness about discussing sex toys. He kept every conversation professional, without inappropriate tones of voice or suggestive words like the guys I'd attempted to date in the past had done.

While I appreciated his emotional distance, disappointment over his lack of interest, except for that one time heat had filled his gaze, pulled me down at the end of every day. It wasn't like I hoped he'd make a pass at me...or did I?

My body and mind warred, but the physical desire for him overran whatever anxious thoughts assaulted me if other people stepped into my personal space.

I spoke with my therapist at length. About my instinctive reaction at shaking Micah's hand but how it hadn't reminded me of my past as other accidental touches by men tended to do. I told her his being in close proximity didn't cut off my oxygen but made my lungs hungrier in a different way.

Desire, she'd suggested, and I didn't bother arguing since she spoke truth.

She said I had to trust myself—not him—to know what was best for me. While he'd given me the opportunity to stretch my boundaries in what I considered a safe environment, I shouldn't do so unless I wanted to.

But Micah didn't push.

Ever.

I looked forward to work with every sunrise. I looked forward to his smiles, his kindness. I also started looking forward to one day taking him up on his offer to touch him again. His suggestion of being available to help me take more steps toward possible healing had clanged loudly in the back of my mind for weeks, and since my therapist hadn't completely shut down the idea, I considered it more with each night that passed.

"I'm firing up the Keurig. Want a coffee?" he asked one afternoon after a very long Monday. He'd been on a call with an unhappy client for over an hour before he was able to finally put the phone down and exit his office. His sandy-blond hair stuck up like he'd been running a hand through it —his typical, sexy look.

"Rough, huh?" I asked, scrunching up my face at the exhaustion lining his.

He sighed and shook his head. "I'm having difficulty finding someone to please Widow Mayfield," he said.

My stomach twisted. I knew she used to book him every other week, but not long after I'd become Elite's secretary, he'd taken his profile off the website. Unsure of why, my mind toyed with all sorts of ridiculous reasons.

"Coffee sounds good." I smiled, hoping to ease him in some way.

Nodding, he turned and ruffled a hand over his thick hair with a heavy sigh.

I touched my bun, which I had wrapped too tight earlier that morning and was giving me a headache. Without a thought, I pulled it loose. I sighed and ran my fingers through the long strands, eyes closing. *So* much better. Why I still felt the need to look all professional when Micah showed up barefoot in jeans and a t-shirt most days, I didn't know.

Dina hadn't ever dressed up to work the office. Had never worn makeup, she'd told me when I'd asked. What was the point when we didn't have clients on site and only the escorts or the two limo drivers ever crossed into my reception area? Was I still trying to impress a man who didn't seem interested in a forbidden office romance?

An ache blossomed in my chest, and I sighed again when I should have been snorting at my fanciful mind.

Sandals and comfy clothes on Wednesday, I promised myself while opening my eyes to get back to work.

Micah stood in the doorway, two mugs in his hands. The heat in his eyes slammed into my chest, knocking that ache into oblivion. While I might not be too familiar with men, the stare he pierced me with couldn't be misunderstood.

"What are you looking at?" I heard myself whisper.

"You let your hair down." His voice dropped lower than usual with a rasp that made my nipples pebble.

The desire to flirt swept through me, heightening my pulse. He was my boss, but there was no denying the draw —or how easily his presence encouraged me to be honest. Open with my thoughts and desires. I wanted him to know me in every way possible.

Ask.

"Do you like it?" I whispered, my face hot and pulse thundering in my ears.

He stared at me, the war in his eyes obvious. A man of integrity, he would want to choose right rather than crossing the lines our roles in the office dictated. The muscle in his jaw clenched. "Yes," he finally said, his voice quiet.

The clock on the wall ticked in my ears. I wanted to make a move but, being a chickenshit, couldn't.

Too much of a gentleman—or perhaps out of concern for me—Micah didn't either. He cleared his throat and handed me one of the coffees.

I eyed his fingertips cradling the mug.

Do it.

Swallowing hard, I reached for the handle, brushing my index finger against his. My breath caught as good old anxiety shot adrenaline through my system. Rather than squeezing tight, my lungs reacted, filling with a rush of oxygen instead.

Micah released his hold, and my hand shook, almost

spilling the coffee. "Okay?" he asked, blue eyes warm and attentive while watching my reaction.

I made a noise of agreement. My heart galloped as I smiled at him. "Thank you."

His sudden grin caused my stomach to swoop. "You're welcome." With a wink, he disappeared into his office.

Blowing out a slow exhale, I sat back in my chair, cradling the mug he'd held in his hands. Steam rose to my nose, and I closed my eyes, inhaling until my chest threatened to burst.

I'd touched him without losing my shit.

It took a few seconds for my smile to ease enough that I could take a sip.

Chapter 7

Micah

I wanted to cross lines so fucking badly.

She'd touched my hand on Monday, intentionally. Her lungs had gasped for air but in the kind of way that suggested instantaneous arousal rather than anxiety. I'd hightailed it to my office before I suggested she do it again.

Sitting with her at lunch on Wednesday, I watched her eat. Her lips open and close. Her tongue flit out to catch a droplet of soft drink that leaked from her straw.

A constant semi filled my jeans whenever I was in her presence, and I imagined taking her in every which way, in every room of my house. I spilled more spunk than I had in my teenage years.

But I didn't touch her. Didn't initiate.

"What are you thinking?"

I ripped my focus off her pink mouth, realizing she'd almost finished her Italian sub when I'd barely eaten any of my cheese steak. Clearing my throat didn't help the heat I could feel creeping over my cheeks.

"Wait." Jasmine huffed a little laugh. "Are you...embarrassed?"

Rolling my eyes, I lifted my head. I raised an eyebrow.

She smirked. "Don't give me that look." Her napkin hit me in the face, and we both laughed. "Tell me."

"Tell you what?" I stalled.

"What made you flush just now."

"You don't want to know." I took a bite of my sub to keep from having to talk.

She eyed me as though trying to read my thoughts. Good luck with that.

Jasmine toyed with a length of hair hanging over her shoulder, and I honed in on the action, breathing deep for a scent of freshness and flowers.

She flirted with me.

The little minx.

I lifted my focus to her face again but didn't lift my brow in question. I simply stared. Pink staining her cheekbones as I studied her in the suddenly tense silence. "What do you want, Jasmine?" I asked, breaking before she did.

"I...I'm not sure." She glanced away, dropping her hand from her hair.

"Hey."

Her focus flitted back to me.

"I'll follow your cues," I murmured. "Always."

The tip of her tongue flicked out over her lower lip, and I bit back a groan. "Can we...be friends?"

"I'd like to think that we already are."

"I mean..." she waved her hand over the table we'd shared a lot in the previous couple of weeks. "More than business talk. I'd like to know things about you."

"Okay." I wiped my mouth and pushed my sub away, crossing my arms across the table. "What about?"

Her mouth opened, and she snapped it shut.

Chuckling, I took pity on her. "My name is Micah

Jonathan Fox. I'm thirty-six years old, love fast cars, making money, and living every day to its fullest. I don't have a dog although I've always wanted one. I can do without cats—allergic—and the idea of a hairless one makes me shudder. Red is my favorite color, I love lobster but am partial to king crab legs. I'm not a huge fan of snow, so I splurged on a place in Cancun where I escape for a few weeks every winter. I watch sports and listen to talk radio probably more than I should, enjoy a horror flick on occasion, and believe it or not—I'll nab one of my mom's romance novels when I'm feeling all sentimental and shit."

"You forgot about your nightlife."

I barked a laugh, loving how Jasmine had propped her chin in her hand, elbow resting atop the table while I spilled a bunch of worthless shit about my life. "That's not something friends discuss."

She lifted an eyebrow like I was fond of doing, and I laughed again.

"Tell me about you."

"I'm twenty-four, have two big sisters, my parents are conservative and protective...I too read romance novels and want a dog. I hate cats—they've got too much of an attitude. I like the snow but not the cold, and I've never been outside of the country although I dream about traveling the world. I see a therapist for my touch issues every other week, and she says I ought to take you up on your offer to help test myself."

Well. Shock me mute.

Jasmine slid her gaze over my face, stopping at my lips.

I held my breath.

"I think one of these days I just might," she murmured.

It took me a few seconds to gather my thoughts and find my voice. "Whenever and wherever."

She smiled, lifting her attention to my eyes again. "I like talking with you."

"I like you too—*talking*." The fuck was wrong with me?

Jasmine shook my foundation, riled me up in ways no other woman had done.

One corner of her lips rose as though she was aware of my...discomfort. She seemed to like it too.

"Come on—back to work we go," I muttered, wrapping up the rest of my sub.

We headed out to my car without another word, and I opened her door. She went to step around me, and her elbow bumped against mine. Her gaze jerked up to my face, but I held still.

A wobbly smile, a hint of surprise and pleasure in her pale eyes sent an ache through my chest.

"Okay?" I rasped the word, more shaken than I'd ever been by the mere brush of arms.

Jasmine hesitated a second before answering, her smile growing brighter. "Yes. I am."

I grinned. "Glad to hear it. Now get your fine ass in my car so we can head back to work."

She squeaked and slid onto the passenger seat.

I slammed the door and walked around the front of my car, realizing what I'd said. "Fuck," I muttered to myself. *Get ahold of yourself, Fox.*

Jasmine sat prim and proper as I started up the car and pulled out of the deli's parking lot. "So. That just happened."

I glanced over to find her face still flushed.

"Sorry. My comment was totally inappropriate."

"But true?"

Her gaze bored into me. *Shit.* Clearing my throat, I

faced forward, watching where I drove. "In my opinion, yes."

"Well, then." She sounded entirely too pleased by my answer.

My hand rested on the stick shift, fingers itching to reach for her thigh. Jaw clenched, I kept my focus on the road.

A flicker light as a feather ghosted over my knuckles.

I glanced down to find Jasmine pulling her hand back from mine. She smiled—appeared so damn pleased with herself I didn't even bother asking if she was all right.

"So, that just happened," I echoed her words from moments earlier.

"Yes." She owned the word. "Yes, it did."

We both grinned all the way back to the office.

Two hours later, I couldn't find a file in my desk. "Jasmine!" I called through my open office door. "Do you know where those applications that came in last week are?"

I still hunted for a sadist to match with the widow.

Jasmine appeared in my doorway, catching my breath as always. She held what I'd been looking for.

"Thanks." I reached for the file folder, and Jasmine released her hold before I had grasped it.

Papers fell.

"Shit." She dropped to her knees, and I pushed back my chair to help gather them from the floor.

Our heads bumped.

We both laughed, and I glanced up to check in with her.

"I'm good," she said, smiling at me as she'd done after touching my hand in the car.

Gazes locked, we reached for a paper at the same time— my fingers brushed over her wrist.

Jasmine blinked and fell backward onto her ass.

"Ah, fuck. Sorry." I hopped up, offering my hand. "Shit." I rubbed my palm down my jeans.

She didn't breathe.

"Jasmine." Her face had paled, and cursing, I once more dropped to the ground beside her, giving her plenty of space. "Hey—look at me."

Pale green eyes peered at me but didn't focus.

"You're alright. Be a good girl and fill those lungs up for me—please, Jasmine."

A small inhale stuttered, lifting her breasts.

"Good." I smiled, wishing I could touch her, wishing like *fuck* I knew what had caused her issues so I could be more careful. "Just like that—again."

She obeyed.

"Put your head between your knees, okay? Let's count and breathe together."

We got through her episode while I cursed myself inside and out. What had set her off that time when she'd been perfectly fine in my car?

Jasmine breathed easily, and she tilted her head, resting her cheek on her upturned knee to face me.

"Better?" I asked, keeping my voice quiet, trying to appear and sound as unintimidating as possible.

"Yeah." A heavy sigh deflated her. "Sorry."

"There's nothing to be sorry for. It was an accident."

She closed her eyes, and it physically hurt to not draw her into my arms and comfort her like I would a sub who'd come down from a high. Hers had been a major low but required the same fucking care.

I hated that I couldn't give it to her.

"Baby steps, sweet secretary of mine."

She huffed an exhale and straightened. "Guess this is

going to be more like a merengue with steps backward on occasion rather than perfect pirouettes across a stage."

"I enjoy dancing," I tossed out, hoping to make her smile.

It worked.

Chapter 8

Jasmine

Ricky, one of Elite's drivers checked in late on Friday afternoon.

His limo had broken down, and I scrambled to find something else since Micah was on the phone with his little brother Sean behind his closed door, hollering more often than not.

It took me over a half-hour, keeping me in the office after five, but Ricky and his escort headed into Boston while I made another call to explain their tardiness to the woman expecting them.

Normally, Micah dealt with such situations, personally getting in touch with the clients to ensure no bumps in the road caused issues. I hoped he didn't mind that I'd taken care of the problem since his brother kept him on the phone.

I turned off my computer and slipped my feet back into my sandals. Moving around the room, I shut the two windows and gathered my stuff.

The rumbling of Micah's voice quieted, and I waited a few more seconds before calling out my usual good night when I left before him.

His door opened, and he glanced at the purse in my hand. "Heading out?"

"Yes." I explained about Ricky and that I'd called the client. "I didn't want to interrupt you. I hope that's okay."

"As long as everything turned out all right, I'm happy."

I didn't turn to leave as I ought to.

I'm off the clock. I'm not his employee right now, am I?

We'd stepped past the boundaries in becoming friends over the past week, but I hadn't attempted to test my luck since losing my shit over spilled papers and an accidental touch. But it had been to my wrist...

Talk about taking steps backward after moving forward so damn easily. I'd gotten down on myself. Allowed a hint of depression to creep in and keep me from trying again.

Micah hadn't questioned me or pushed for information for which I was thankful. The small freak-out had brought back up my past a bit, and I hated the setback.

He shoved his hands in his jeans pockets. "Do you want to stay for dinner?"

Warmth sprang to life between my thighs, and my heart jumped. He hadn't initiated anything, ever, but I wasn't about to pass up an opportunity to spend time with him outside the office. Maybe I would get brave again. "S-Sure."

Tipping his head toward the door leading into his home, he smiled. "Come on in."

For the first time since I'd started working for him two months earlier, I walked over the threshold of the Fox's lair. While I'd seen the living room beyond, I'd never had the gall to snoop when he went out of town.

Warm colors, leather, paintings, a wide stone fireplace... definitely a man's home, but inviting. Soothing, I figured, but at that moment, my blood rushed, and thoughts fluttered around like a bunch of dive-bombing bats gobbling up mosquitoes.

"Have a seat," he said.

I shot a text off to my mom, telling her I had to work late so she wouldn't worry, and climbed onto a barstool at the massive island dominating his chef's kitchen. Stainless-steel appliances gleamed, and the granite countertops were cluttered with high-end gadgets.

Micah moved around the kitchen, gathering things from the fridge and cabinets. "Do you cook?" he asked, his back to me.

Appreciating the muscles rippling beneath his tight T-shirt, I swallowed. "A little."

"I started using Healthy Chef a couple of weeks ago."

"Those meals-in-a-box businesses were a great idea for whoever thought it up. Is their food any good?"

"So far." He glanced over his shoulder. "Want to help?"

"Sure." I slid off the stool and rubbed my damp palms down my skirt.

"Why don't you pour us some wine, and we'll dive into the recipe together and see if we can hit it out of the park."

Jitters still jumped in my stomach, but my hands were steady while I filled two glasses he'd pulled from the corner cabinet.

I held the stem of the half-full glasses and offered him one. My heart sped as he glanced down at my fingers.

He lifted his gaze, one eyebrow raised as though asking permission to touch me. "May I?"

Leave it up to a Dom to verbalize consent.

Breathe snagged, I nodded.

"Words, Jasmine."

"Y-Yes." I gulped and watched his hand reach toward mine. The glass shook in my hold.

Micah's pinkie brushed over one of my fingertips.

A zap of lightning lit my body—and tightened my chest.

"Jasmine?" His gaze filled with concern.

I held up a hand and closed my eyes, focusing on breathing.

Micah began counting, and I followed along with his instructions, eased in submitting to his lead. In less than a minute, my lungs relaxed.

"I'm okay." I met his gaze, my smile wobbling. "Shortest recovery time ever."

He continued watching me as though checking I spoke the truth.

Needing to escape his intense stare that warmed me between the thighs, I turned my attention to the stuff he'd gotten from the fridge and cabinets. "So what are we making tonight?" My voice wasn't exactly steady, but Micah got the hint I was ready to move on.

"Pan-seared scallops and some funky-looking veggies."

I snickered.

"Here." He pushed the vegetables my way. "You can cut, and I'll heat up the pan to sauté them."

I headed over to the sink to wash my hands.

"So." The weight of his stare settled on the side of my face a few minutes later, but I focused on finishing chopping the veggies like he'd told me to do. "Would you mind my asking what caused your inability to handle a person touching you? I'll admit the not knowing is driving me insane, especially after that little episode the other day. And, before you toss out an excuse about being on the clock, we're not at work right now. I'm not your boss, and you aren't my employee. We're just two friends making dinner together."

Friends. I wished we could be a hell of a lot more. And

gaining any ground with him meant sharing what few people knew about. I could trust Micah with the truth.

The thought of the foster boy who'd spent time in our house while I was a tween twisted my stomach as it always did when he came to mind, but no hint of panic rose. My breathing remained steady and calm.

"My parents used to take in foster kids when I was younger." I placed the cutting board and knife in the sink without glancing at Micah. "Billy behaved like the perfect big brother, looking out for Dina, Liz, and me. The first time he came into my room at night, I thought he was sleep walking."

I went silent for a few minutes while washing the two items, making sure anxiety wasn't secretly lying in wait to rise up and choke off my air.

"Does it help or hurt to talk about it?" Micah asked when I didn't continue.

I peered over at him for a few seconds, appreciating the concern in his eyes. "I've gone to countless therapists but haven't ever told anyone outside of my family. And the police, of course."

"You don't have to talk about it if you don't want to. I just...want to know what sets you off so I never do it. I hate seeing you in a panic like that."

I wanted to be morose and tell him to get used to it, but Micah genuinely cared. And seeing as how we were friends and would spend months and maybe even years together three days a week, he ought to be aware of the whole story.

Maybe talking about it more often *would* help with the healing too. I chewed on the inside of my lip while drying my hands but figured to hell with it. I was desperate to move on with my life and wasn't above trying whatever might initiate forward motion. Drawing a deep breath, I hung up the towel and began.

Letting go of the long-ass story to someone other than a therapist released tension in my body I hadn't realized I carried. Micah didn't interrupt as I spilled the shit of my past, and his eyes weren't overflowing with pity when I glanced his way once we sat to eat, wondering what he thought.

I didn't go deep into details, but it had been enough that an older boy would have been tossed behind bars for what he'd done. Grabbing my wrists to hold me still while he ground his dick over my backside being the worst of it—and the most triggering.

Micah and I discussed my therapy. The couple of times men had accidentally bumped into me at the grocery store, the mall, and while in college where I attempted to gain some education on business so I would make a good secretary.

"You're the best I've ever had."

My gaze snapped up off my empty plate, and I finished chewing my last bite of scallop while studying his face for bullshit.

"I'm serious. You're one hell of a right hand in helping me run my business."

Warmth flooded me from my hair follicles atop my head to my toenails. "Thank you."

He grinned and stood, taking both our plates without touching me. "Just don't tell Dina I said that."

I snorted and followed him back into the kitchen. "She's got one hell of a temper."

"Damn right," he muttered his agreement while setting our plates in the sink.

"If Billy had actually...raped me, she would have

stabbed him with a pitchfork."

I expected laughter, but his lips thinned, and he grasped the edge of the counter a brief moment before retrieving the opened bottle of wine sitting on the island.

"I have zero tolerance for assholes like that." Anger laced Micah's voice. "I understand the whole juvie thing, but stalking you years later and threatening you after you filed restraining orders?" He shook his head, the muscle in his jaw ticking as he poured himself more wine. "The fucker ought to be shot." Micah gestured to the glass I held in my hand, but I shook my head.

"At least I'm getting better," I said, fingering the two inch scar beneath my left ear that *had* landed Billy's ass in jail. "I *know* I am. I mean, look at me." A huff of laughter left my lungs. "I'm alone with a man in his kitchen, less than three feet from him, and I'm not freaking out."

I also wanted a hell of a lot more with said man.

"I'm happy for you." Warmth filled his steady gaze. "And me, if you don't mind me being truthful?"

Tingles of heat slid through my veins, igniting desire in my core as it always did when Micah studied me with his intense stare. "Always. I appreciate honesty."

His slow smile was deadly. Tempting. "Living room?"

"Sounds good." I followed him on shaky legs and settled onto the couch.

He sat in a recliner across from me.

Since we'd crossed the line into friendship, and he'd gone with speaking the truth, I decided to lay my cards on the coffee table between us too. "It *is* because of you that I feel I'm making progress, you know," I said, my pulse thrumming at my confession.

"How so?" he asked, lifting his wine glass to sip.

Pulling up my big girl panties, I went for it. "You are the

first person to make me crave physical interaction. I've read about it, talked about it with my sisters regarding their experiences, but not once have I wanted or felt comfortable enough to think of someone touching me."

Chapter 9

Micah

Jesus.

I almost choked on my wine. If the look in her eyes wasn't an invitation, I wasn't a Dom with fifteen years of experience under my belt. I cleared my throat and set the glass aside. Tense silence zapped between us, but she didn't lower her head like usual whenever she seemed uncomfortable. Her green eyes peered at me with a hint of question. Insecurity. But pupils dominated her pale irises, and the pulse jumped in her neck.

Sure, she'd had a slight setback after giving me permission to touch her hand wrapped around the wine glass, but she'd bounced back quickly. I wanted to help—lusted for it. But talking things through always came first for me before getting involved.

"Have you dreamed about me touching you?" I asked.

"Yes," she whispered without hesitation—almost as if desperate for me to push her boundaries and ask for more.

My dick twitched to life.

I wouldn't do what her eyes suggested she craved in a physical sense, but I wasn't about to pass up the opportunity she gifted me. Discussion might help break down barriers and allow for greater trust. And I would enjoy every fucking bit of information I could get past her lips to jerk off to later.

"How?"

"You mean how do you touch me in my dreams?" Her low, husky voice rushed blood to my cock, but I didn't bother trying to hide the fact she turned me on. Honesty, and all that shit.

"Yes."

"Gently." She swallowed but held my gaze with surprising strength for an innocent. "With your fingertips until I grow accustomed to the feeling."

"Where?" My voice sounded strangled as my self-control wavered at the images flashing through my mind.

"Here." She lifted her hand and glanced at her upright palm.

Fuck my usual stance on spontaneity being a hard limit for me. I needed to fucking know, and if my Dom instincts were any good—which they fucking were—I was well aware of how to get her submissive side to comply.

Consensually, of course.

She could deny me, and I would submit to her having the power in that moment.

"If I ask anything you aren't comfortable answering, just say so. Okay?"

She nodded.

"I need words, Jasmine."

"Yes," she whispered.

"Where else do I touch you? Put your wine down and show me." I used my Dom voice and relaxed back into my recliner, legs spread, giving her an eyeful of the hard ridge lining my jeans.

Her attention drifted down between my thighs, her lips parting on a sharp inhale.

Fucking hell, this woman.

Trembling, she set the wine glass on the table beside her as though her brain linked directly to my command. When she sat back, she uncrossed her legs but kept her knees pressed together, the darkness beneath her casual skirt beckoning to me. "H-Here." She slowly trailed her fingers up her arm, over her collarbone where she lingered. Up her neck and with painstaking hesitancy over her lips.

I groaned. "Where else, Jasmine?"

She swallowed, gaze still on my cock, and ran her hand back down her neck and over the swell of her breasts.

"Show me." My tone held firm, and she followed the request without hesitation, slipping her hand up inside her tank top. Lower lip between her teeth, she squirmed on the couch, same as when I'd caught her drooling over sex toys online.

"Is my touch still gentle?" I asked, my attention glued to the hand moving beneath her shirt, hiding one of the hard nipples pressing against the cotton.

"N-Not so much." Her needy tone brought another groan to my lips.

Christ.

"Where else do I put my hands on you in your dreams?"

Face red, she closed her eyes.

"Jasmine?" I checked in. "We can stop if you want."

"N-No!" She shook her head quickly. "You suck on my breasts. Bite my nipples." The words rushed from her, filling my head with curses.

I swallowed hard. "And do you like it? That little bit of pain?"

"Yes," she gasped and clenched her legs together as

she played with her breasts. "Sometimes...sometimes I imagine you use clamps on them." She nibbled on her lower lip.

I'd never wanted a woman so much in my fucking life. Blood pulsed in my ears, my dick. I peered at the darkness beneath her skirt, my cock aching. "Are you turned on right now?"

She whimpered and nodded, still chewing on that goddamned lip I wanted to soothe with my tongue.

"Jasmine?"

"Yes?" she breathed, finally gifting me the sight of her pupil-blown eyes. Not one ounce of fear or wariness rested in her gaze. Nothing but desire radiated from her.

"Where else do I touch you?"

"D-Down there."

Fuck yes I would, given the chance.

"Lift your skirt so I can see how wet you are." Every muscle in my body tensed to move, but I held myself still, expecting her to put a stop to what I pushed for.

A full body tremor rippled over her—but she didn't hesitate to shimmy her skirt up to her hips. White panties hid her pussy from my view.

I groaned, and she moaned as though the noise coming from me pulsed need through her core.

With one finger, she skimmed down the lace darkened with wetness.

"Goddamn." I clutched at the recliner's armrests.

She slid her fingertip beneath the edge of her panties and rubbed up over her clit, a gasp parting her lips and tipping her head back.

I found myself stroking my cock through my jeans. Jasmine might be an innocent in the physical sense, but her mind? That thing of beauty was a different story.

But how far would she go? How much trust had I earned? How much honesty would she allow between us?

"Do I make you come in your dreams, Jasmine?" My tone was wrecked with lust, husky and broken.

"Yes," she whispered, eyes clenched shut.

"Let me see your pretty pussy."

With one hand, she pulled her panties to the side. Her pink, swollen labia glistened beneath a thatch of blonde curls.

Drooling, I stroked myself and stared as she pressed two fingers into her pussy.

She whimpered, slowly fucking herself, hips grinding her core against her palm.

"I want to watch you come, Jasmine," I offered her my truth, lifting my attention to her face as little noises flew past her parted lips. "Open your eyes and look at me."

Panting, she did as told, hazed, pale eyes peering at me —but *seeing* me.

"Imagine those fingers fucking into your needy pussy are mine," I murmured, knowing my words would make or break the scene we were indulging in.

A sharp inhale lifted her chest, and her back bowed off my couch, giving me what I wanted. "O-Oh!" Her breath caught again, and she shuddered, crying out. The sounds of wet finger fucking caused my mouth to flood with drool. Cream covered her fingers, and I squeezed my cock to keep from blowing my load in my jeans.

"Jesus, Jasmine." My blood rushed and my ears rang as she slowly settled.

Her breasts heaved with every aftershock rippling through her flushed body.

"If you ever decide you want me to touch you for real," I rasped, "you only need to ask."

Praying to God she would beg right then and there, I held my breath the best my pounding heart allowed.

Face growing a deeper shade of red, she wiped her fingers off on her panties and tugged her skirt back into place. "I should go," she whispered, her gaze on the floor.

Fuck, fuck, fuck.

"Jasmine."

Her breath caught again, and she clutched her hands on her lap, but she lifted her head. Conflicting emotions warred in her eyes, clenching up my insides.

"Are you okay?"

She nodded.

"You sure? I need words."

"Yes." A small smirk lifted her lips even though her eyes didn't lighten from the intensity that had rolled in from sharing her secrets and climaxing in front of me. "More than okay, actually."

My shoulders relaxed, and I returned her smile even though my balls fucking ached. I'd pushed her too hard but couldn't find a single fuck to give since she didn't end up panicking. "I'm not sorry about what just happened."

"Neither am I."

Our upturned lips flatlined as we stared at each other, the antique clock on the mantle ticking away without a care in the world. I wanted to tell her that I was serious about my offer. I lusted to get on my knees and beg her to let me touch her. Grovel, plead...fuck, did I desire to feel her soft flesh beneath my hands.

Self-control, Fox.

I managed to stay in my seat regardless of the yearning attempting to take over my mind.

"I'll see you next week?" I finally broke the silence

between us, needing to know that everything was good between us.

A smile lifted her lips and made me think of kissing. Tasting her tongue.

Fucking hell.

"Of course," she murmured.

I released the breath I hadn't realized I'd held. Clearing my throat, I stood. "I'll walk you out."

She glanced at my straining cock, and fuck me, if she didn't lick her lips and tempt me to the breaking point.

Groaning, I motioned toward the door. "Come on, before I go back on my promise I'm really hating myself for right now."

Lower lip between her teeth, she scurried into the kitchen and grabbed her purse, letting me know that hard limit of physical touch still sat in place.

"Are you okay to drive?" I asked, leading her out the front door.

"I only drank the one glass of wine. I'm fine."

I shoved my hands in my pockets once we reached her car and stepped back out of her way rather than crowding in close and attacking her mouth. "Be careful. Drive safe."

"I'm always careful." She climbed into her car. It roared to life, but she hesitated, hands on the steering wheel, peering at me through the driver's side window.

I nodded toward the driveway and mouthed, "Go."

Fingers fluttering my way, she backed away, leaving me aching. Her taillights disappeared, and I turned toward the house, bypassing the dirty dishes and my wine.

Hot water rained on me in my shower seconds later, and a handful of strokes down my cock drew up my balls and shot ropes of cum against the tiled wall.

My release wasn't nearly as satisfying as I'd hoped. I still ached for Jasmine—and not just in my groin. My chest actually hurt with the need to know her more, and while thrilled I'd gotten to see her come, those few moments of intimacy together weren't nearly enough to sate my lust for her.

Chapter 10

Jasmine

I was desperate for Micah's hands on my skin.

Anxiety, my old friend, hadn't reared its ugly head in the aftermath of what we'd done even as he had walked me to my car. I hadn't wanted to leave. I'd considered climbing back out and testing myself further, but he'd told me to go.

Masturbating in front of Micah was the hottest, most insane thing I'd ever done in my twenty-four years, and I lusted for more. *Lots* more. Like a toddler tasting her first lollipop, my mouth watered, and I wanted to throw a tantrum until I got what would satisfy my craving. The memory of the heat in his eyes, the bulge in his jeans made me whimper.

I pulled into my parents' driveway almost two hours later than my usual time, my pussy throbbing again. The second I climbed from the car, a shiver pebbled my skin even though summertime heat lingered and licked over my flushed skin in the early evening's night air.

I glanced around our neighborhood while slinging my purse over my shoulder, the back of my neck tingling. My feet moved as fast as my thumping heart, and I locked the front door behind me. Another shiver sent a tremor down through my body.

"Jasmine? That you?" Mom called from the kitchen.

Drawing a deep breath, I told myself to calm down. "Yes, Mom."

"Sorry you had to work late," she said. "I saved a plate for you."

"I-I grabbed something on the way home." Lying hadn't ever been an issue for me, but I didn't want to share what I'd been up to. Even though I considered hanging with Micah outside work a step in the right direction, Mom would be concerned and probably tell me to be careful in spending time alone with a man—even though three days a week we were all up in each other's business. Sort of.

Pulling my phone from my purse, I headed up the stairs. I chewed on the inside of my lip, considering how inappropriate it would be to text my boss for something besides work. A huffed laugh escaped me. As if we hadn't crossed a serious line earlier.

Thank you, I finally texted once I locked myself in my bedroom.

Leaning against my door, I stared at my phone. The ding caused me to jump.

Micah: **Anytime.**

I groaned and put my phone down so I wouldn't be tempted to text him back, letting him know I wanted to take him up on his offer. Now. Yesterday. Tomorrow. And every day after that for as long as he was willing.

My nerves got the best of me on Monday morning. I unlocked the office and let myself in, my chest tight. Micah's usual presence that pebbled my skin was absent, but the door to his private lair stood open, allowing me unhindered sight into his living room. I didn't catch a glimpse of him.

Hands shaking, I put my purse away and turned on the computer. I punched in the code for the voicemail and struggled to keep my writing legible while jotting down messages and notes of who needed to be called back.

The scent of freshly brewed coffee filtered past my nose, and I hoped for yet dreaded Micah's arrival.

Legs a jelly-like mess, I walked into his office and placed the messages on his desk. He'd already been in—his computer hummed, and an open client's folder and pen lay atop his desk. He never left unfinished business like that.

I returned to my office and glanced out into his living room once more. "Micah?"

He didn't answer, and I wrung my hands, wondering where he'd gotten to. Shaking my head, I sat back at my desk and forced myself to focus on getting the payroll started early. Twenty silent, tense minutes later, the sound of his footsteps finally reached my straining ears.

"Morning," he said, his low voice sending a shudder through my body.

I turned toward the door and smiled, my heart pounding. "Morning."

He went barefoot as usual when having no plans to leave the office that day, jeans, and an entirely too-tight T-shirt beautifully fitted to showcase his muscles.

I wanted to touch. Lusted for it ten times worse than before we'd shared a type of intimacy in his living room three nights earlier.

"I brought you a coffee," he said, his gaze flitting over my shorts and tank top. Appreciation blazed in his eyes. Guess that boss/employee line we had crossed had filtered into the office.

I could live with that. Desired it more than was appropriate.

"Thanks," I whispered, my pulse thrumming.

He held the mug out to me, eyebrow raised the same as it had been on Monday night, his hand clasped around the entire thing.

It was my turn to initiate—if I wanted to, his gaze stated. *Do it.*

My entire body shook, but I brushed my fingers across his while taking the coffee. Electricity raced over my skin, and I sucked in my lower lip to keep needy noises from escaping while setting the coffee down before I spilled it.

"Are you okay?" he asked, studying me closely with heat in his eyes that made me damp between the thighs.

Was I?

My fast breaths came unrestricted. My heart pounded. My usual panic was nowhere to be found.

Lightness flooded my chest, and although I shook like a leaf during a storm, I smiled. "Yes."

"Sweet." Grinning, he ambled away. "I'll be in my office if you need anything."

I slumped back in my chair, biting my tongue to keep my giggles contained. I had intentionally touched Micah like I'd done in his car without losing my shit. Fist to my mouth to remain quiet, I decided I wanted to try again—as soon as I got the chance.

The morning sped past in a blur of numbers, phone calls, and files. My face hurt from smiling, but by five, my nerves returned enough to bring back the jitters in my stomach.

Micah had acted the professional boss all day long. We'd even gone out to grab a sub together for lunch, but he kept his distance. No sexual innuendos or inappropriate questions. No suggestive offers to help me take the next step.

I shut down my computer, heart in my throat, and moved into his open doorway. "I'm heading out," I somehow managed to get passed my lips.

He glanced at his watch and lifted his head to meet my gaze. "Come here."

My legs shook as I obeyed, but he rolled back on his chair and spun, motioning me around the desk rather than in front of it.

I stopped a couple feet away from his knees, heat racing through my body, settling between my thighs.

Micah lifted his hand toward me, fingers splayed, and peered up at me.

The chicken part of me wanted to turn and take off. The woman part of me, the desire to heal and move forward in my quest for normalcy, kept me from running. He wasn't initiating touch to pull me closer. He offered his hand for me to test myself. His stance, the look in his eyes told me it was my decision as was every submissive's right when in a scene with a Dom.

I wondered how much it cost him to relinquish control. Since I'd become somewhat of an expert on the BDSM lifestyle in knowledge only, I knew the power he offered me in that moment went outside his norm.

Micah was definitely a Dom who could be trusted—he'd proven that to me on Friday night when a lesser man with a similar raging hard-on would have leapt over the coffee table to take advantage of me. Dina had assured me about his ethics and kindness, and I wanted to believe he would treat me right no matter our situation. He would be gentle until I asked for something more. Take his time because I gravitated toward hesitancy with good reason he now understood.

Stepping closer, my gaze latched on his hand, I lifted my own. I brushed a fingertip across his wrist, and a shot of that same electric-charged energy crackled down through my body straight to my clit. I held my breath and slowly slid my finger down across his palm, to the tip of his middle finger.

I stepped back, my exhale leaving in a rush as I dropped my hand to my side.

"Are you okay?" he checked in with me like a good Dom would, same as he always did, his voice gruff, almost...strangled.

"Yes," I whispered, desire and need evident in my tone. I didn't care he probably read me like an open book.

"Would you like to touch me again?"

Chewing on the inside of my lip, I nodded, a hell of a lot more than *want* pushing me to try for more.

Micah gripped his arm rests as though locking himself in place, letting me know with the action that he would keep his hands to himself, same as he'd done on Friday. "Go ahead. My promise stands...until you ask me otherwise."

Heart racing, I stepped to his side rather than between his spread thighs and reached out to run my fingers over the mussed hair atop his head like I'd been dying to do. "Silky soft," I heard myself murmur while smiling. I'd expected crunchy with product.

Micah lifted his head, his gaze on my lips, and I moved my fingertips over his smooth forehead.

He sighed but continued to peer up at me, that energy still crackling, heating my blood until it pulsed between my thighs.

I slid my light touch down his temple to his close-clipped sideburn.

"Not quite as silky," I said on a half-giggle of pure nerves bordering on losing my shit. My fingers continued as if on their own, along his scruffy jaw to his chin. I paused, my gaze glued to his lips, my smile fading.

Wetness soaked my panties. My pulse thrummed in my ears, and I wanted nothing more than to kiss him. Taste a man's lips for the very first time. Intimacy like I'd never known—had only been able to dream about thanks to Billy.

My hand fell away at his name in my thoughts, and I shuffled back a couple of steps. Ears suddenly ringing, I drew a deep breath, thankful at least that my chest didn't tighten. "I-I need to go," I heard myself say.

"I'll walk you out." Micah stood, and I spun, counting in as I breathed. Counting down as I exhaled.

"Jasmine?"

I grabbed my purse off the desk and stopped, eyes clenched shut.

"Are you okay?"

"Yes. J-Just reached my limit for the day." A burst of the half-hysterical laughter flew from my lips, and I clasped a hand over my mouth.

Micah moved in closer as if to reach for me on instinct, but I stepped back and shook my head.

"I-I'm fine," I said, my voice unsteady as I clutched at the strap of my purse.

He peered at me, hands fisted at his sides, brow furrowed. "You're sure?"

I inhaled until my lungs burned and let the air escape until my shoulders slumped. "Yes."

With a single nod, he moved to the office door and opened it. The sun still shone hot, waves shimmering up from his tarred driveway, heating through my flip-flops in a matter of seconds.

"Goddamn, it's stifling out here," he grumbled.

I climbed into my car and turned it on, lowering all of the windows to let the heat out while the AC cranked up. "Thank you, Micah."

His smile appeared pained. I expected from the massive bulge between his thighs I tried like hell to ignore. "Like I said, anytime."

Chapter 11

Micah

I wanted to rip her shorts off and fuck her against the wall—the door—on the floor. Hell, I just wanted inside of her sweet body. Those damn cutoffs, cute little top that hugged her curves. Flip-flops beneath her pink-painted toenails. She'd even started leaving her hair down since the day I'd said I liked it.

Golden waves wafted her sweet perfume every time she moved her head.

Goddamn, something had to give. Celibate for over two months, and I'd been jerking off so damn much that *both* my wrists ached.

Jasmine had taken some major steps in recovery since meeting me, but how far would she go before her mind shut her down to the point of a panic attack like the two she'd experienced with me? She'd talked herself down from one after touching my face. She'd held on, and I couldn't have been more proud of her—and worried.

I wanted her, but I cared about her recovery more than my own needs. Jasmine came first, and I could wait.

She would be worth the suffering of blue balls.

I hoped.

Friday morning, I rushed to get all of my work buttoned up for the weekend. At noon, I poked my head out of my office door. "Let's shut down the office at two today and get the hell out of here."

"Oh." She turned from her desk.

"Late lunch," I offered in way of explanation for our leaving early for the day. "Care to join me?"

"A company meeting?"

I grinned. "How about a date since we'll be off the clock?"

Pink flushed her cheeks. "Okay."

The next two hours dragged, and my knee bounced under my desk as I went through the weekend's schedule and the mass of clients Elite had lined up. Once sure everything should be set for the night, I shut down my computer, programmed the office phone to forward to my cell, and hurried out to the reception area.

"Ready?"

Jasmine nodded and gathered her things.

We walked out into the heat, and I grimaced. "We're going someplace nice that has good air-conditioning."

She laughed. "You don't like summer?"

"I do, but these heat waves suck ass."

Her continued laughter tingled through my chest, and I smiled. We went to the North End and devoured a basket of freshly baked bread along with the manicotti we'd both ordered in the cool, brick basement of a family-owned Italian restaurant. Cups of coffee and tiramisu sat in front of us as we lingered, chatting about the mundane things in life. What annoyed us. What made us laugh out loud.

My little brother Sean answered both of those questions for me.

"Do you see him often?" she asked and slid her fork into the dessert we'd agreed to share.

"Every couple of weeks he and some of my friends get together for whichever sport is on. Once a month, I have him and my parents over for dinner too."

"I wish I had a little brother."

"No you don't," I assured her and stared as she put the fork in her mouth, her lips closing over the bite of tiramisu.

"Mmm." Jasmine's eyes closed, and she smiled. "So good..."

My cock twitched, jealous over her mouthful of food.

"You know—" she licked her fork clean and eyed my hand resting on the small table between us "—I keep thinking I imagined touching you the other day in your office."

"And I keep thinking about your cries as you came on my couch," I tossed right back at her, my heart pounding and cock swelling.

Her breath hitched, and she slowly lowered the fork to the table. She glanced around the restaurant, but I didn't give a shit if the other early diners heard our conversation. Her gaze returned to my hand.

"Go ahead." I didn't move but waited for her to take another step.

She bit her lip but fluttered her fingertips over my knuckles.

My dick bucked. Hard.

I held my tongue rather than telling her how much she turned me on with a simple touch. I went for something I hoped would have more of an impact even though it might be pushing or rushing things in a different way. "I would love to have you over some night for dinner with my family."

Her fingers paused as she lifted her head, but she didn't pull her touch away from me. "You want me to meet your parents? And Sean?"

"Yes."

She smiled, her eyes shining in the candle light between us, and her palm lowered to fully rest against the back of my hand. "Okay."

I waited for her breath to catch. Lips to part as she sucked down oxygen into starved lungs.

Neither happened.

"You're touching me," I whispered a reminder in case for some fucked up reason she'd forgotten.

Jasmine's gaze flitted to our hands. She flicked her fingertips over the top of my wrist. "I am," she whispered right back.

"You aren't panicking."

Blue eyes full of hunger and happiness lifted to mine. "I...feel safe with you, Micah. I-I can't promise I won't flip out the next time I touch you, but this...this is good."

Goddamned fucking right it is.

I grinned, suddenly ready to finish up and head out into the heat I couldn't stand. "You going to eat that?" I asked, nodding toward the barely-touched dessert as tingles of need raced up through my arm into my chest.

Jasmine sat back, taking away her touch to put her hand on her stomach. "I want to, but I'm so damn full."

I grabbed my wallet and threw a couple large bills onto the table, surprised I didn't shake. "Let's get out of here."

Chapter 12

Jasmine

Micah pulled his car into his garage and cut the engine. I wasn't quick to climb out, and neither was he. I glanced at the door leading into the house.

"Want to come in?" he said as though reading my mind.

"Yes," I replied without hesitation, enough anticipation in my voice that my face heated. I'd been making huge strides and expected I would have to backpedal at some point again, but I wouldn't find out for sure without continuing to move forward.

And Micah was willing, so...

He let us into the kitchen and tossed his keys onto the island taking up most of the space.

Do it. Go for it.

I stepped close behind him and laid my palm on his shoulder blade. The heat of his skin through the shirt covering his muscles seared my palm as he stilled. Heart racing, I ran my hand across the breadth of his shoulders, my fingers dipping in and around the tense muscles beneath his skin. Down the back of his arm and up again.

He didn't move, simply allowing me to take as much as I wanted.

Emboldened by all the oxygen racing into my lungs, I laid my purse on the island alongside his keys, the warmth of his body caressing the front of mine although we didn't touch.

I reached for the hair atop his head, once more surprised by the softness. Nothing but arousal and desire for more swarmed through me. No anxiety, no nervousness beyond the unknown of what might happen in the following minutes.

Lower lip between my teeth, I traced the shell of his ear with my fingertip.

A shudder rippled down through him, his soft groan making my core clench.

I caressed his neck, and he leaned into my touch as though desperate for more. Unsure of what steps I ought to take next, I moved back, my arm dropping.

Micah finally turned, the fire in his eyes catching my breath. His hands fisted at his sides. "I want you so bad, it hurts," he whispered.

My gaze dropped to the huge bulge in his jeans.

Pulse thundering in my ears, I licked my lips while trying to figure out how to vocalize my thoughts. No anxiety roused, but tension rippled through me.

"You're killing me, Jasmine—tell me what you desire. Anything. It's yours."

"Can I touch you? There?"

"Christ, Jasmine." He swallowed hard. "That's...a little much. Are you sure?"

My insides relaxed at his usual checking in with me.

"Will you keep your hands to yourself?" I asked, lifting my focus to search his eyes. I found what I expected and trusted to find—every time. Heat and honesty.

"I won't go back on my promise, Jasmine," he swore. "Not until you ask me to."

"Then show me."

Micah groaned but unzipped his jeans with shaking hands and reached in, pulling out the thickest cock I'd ever seen. My pussy clenched at the thought of him burying his long length deep inside of me like I'd dreamed about.

Squeezing, he slid his hand down to the base and held himself still.

He gave me full power. Complete control I'd realized I needed to make progress. As long as I was the initiator, I felt sure I wouldn't have a setback.

Unable to look away from the pearl of pre-cum glistening on its tip, I stepped closer. "I'm going to touch you."

"Please," he rasped.

With the pad of my thumb, I rubbed the slippery liquid down the front of his cock and closed my fingers around the other side. I gasped at the feel of him. His skin was hot. Hard, yet silky soft. I tightened my grip and slid my hand back up to the mushroom head, a ripple of arousal fluttering over me.

"I didn't expect it to feel like this," I murmured, transfixed on how he moved through my fist. "Like...satin and steel at the same time. You're beautiful."

He hissed, making my pussy flood with wetness.

"That's so damn good, Jasmine," he groaned but remained still. "God, do I love having your hands on me."

My hands on *him*...definitely an easier step forward than him attempting to touch me.

I slid down his length until my pinkie brushed his fingers still clutching the base of his cock. Back up to smear through the moisture gathering at the tip again and another slick slide to his fingers. The feel of him was addictive.

"Jesus fucking Christ, Jasmine."

Tearing my gaze off his stiff length, I lifted my head. The heat in his gaze sent another rush of fire through me, and I pressed my thighs together. "Am I hurting you?" I whispered, stilling my stroking over his hard flesh.

His strained smile didn't reassure me. "Only in the best way possible."

I squeezed again and stroked, holding his gaze—lost in it, really. His dark blue eyes commanded my full attention.

The muscle in his jaw ticked, and I imagined he wanted to kiss me. Maybe even fuck me right there on the kitchen island. But, he wouldn't—unless I asked him to.

Having that power over him was a heady thing. Addictive.

"Can I kiss you?" I whispered, my focus dropping to his parted lips as my hand once more halted its movements over his length.

Micah nodded and slumped onto the barstool directly behind him, releasing his cock. He sat at eye level...fingers digging into his thighs.

Still holding his hard cock, I stepped between his legs. An unsteady breath filled my lungs, and I leaned forward, closing my eyes.

"Look at me, Jasmine."

Halting my forward motion, I fluttered my eyelashes back up.

"This is a major step—you need to keep your focus on me so you remember who you're touching."

"I-I'll go cross-eyed," I said, on the verge of giggling from nerves and need.

"Then go cross-eyed," he insisted, his low tone liquid

sex, like melted chocolate on my tongue. "I just want you to stay in the present, okay? Seeing me might help—and if you're okay after the first brush of our lips, then go ahead and close your eyes. Try for more. I'm at your disposal."

I studied his eyes, finding no hint of jesting, nothing but genuine desire to help me. And definitely kiss me. "Thank you."

A slow smile curled up one side of his lips. "You can thank me after you kiss me. Go ahead, Jasmine. Take what you want."

Our noses brushed without issue since I initiated it, and I inhaled his sweet breath, emboldened to briefly press my lips to his. My heart rate kicked up even higher but in a good way.

Micah didn't respond, but sat still as stone.

I pulled away, gaze still latched on his. "Kiss me back, Micah," I whispered and squeezed his slick length.

He swallowed audibly and nodded.

I stroked down his cock once then leaned in again but couldn't keep from closing my eyes as his lips moved against mine.

My knees went weak at the gentle yet firm press of his mouth. A rush of warmth slid over me—desire and the furthest thing from anxiety or panic a woman could possibly feel.

I wanted more.

Stepping in closer, I smoothed pre-cum down to his base, and Micah groaned, flicking his tongue along my lips.

The light touch startled me, but I was too worked up to pull back. I opened, letting him in, tasting his tongue in the same way he did mine. Languid, slow strokes roused a craving deep inside me, making everything fade from my mind but him. His flavor. His arousal beneath my hand as I stroked his length in time with our tangling tongues. We shared breaths, quiet moans escaping both of us.

His cock jumped against my palm, and I squeezed again, milking back up and over the leaking head. He was so sticky. Wet.

He leaned away from me and lowered his gaze, his inhales quickening as he thrust up into my hold. "If you don't stop, I'm going to come all over us."

"I want you to," I murmured, mesmerized by the soft yet hard feel and sight of his weeping slit appearing and withdrawing from my fist.

He thrust his hips as I stroked downward. "Jesus—fuck, Jasmine. I'm...I'm not used to giving up this kind of control —you're fucking *killing* me."

I moved my hand in time with his hips, his groans and quiet curses spurring me on, pulling my focus toward his face.

Panting, he watched where I touched him, pink flushing his high cheekbones. Tongue flicking out to lick his lower lip as though he thirsted for more. "Your hand on me...fucking amazing, Jasmine. So damn good. I'm so fucking close."

My core pulsed, and I bit back a whimper.

"Gonna—" he gasped out, spine arching, entire body going taut.

"Come for me," I whispered, gaze dropping to the swelling head rubbing up through my palm and fingers.

"Aw, fuck!"

White cum shot in an arch from his cock, landing on my forearm with singeing heat. I hadn't realized I'd moved so tight against him, my hips pressing on the inside of his thighs as he jerked and squirted onto his shirt and my hand.

I lifted my head to find him staring at me as he shuddered through his climax. Desire slammed into me, and I kissed him without thought, working him until he pulled back, gasping.

"Too much," he explained, his voice wrecked.

I stilled, his words settling over me.

"I want to touch you so bad," he murmured before I could back away, his hands still clutching at his thighs.

He hadn't meant what we'd done was *too much*. My touch had gone beyond comfortable. The fact he wanted to return the favor turned my insides to liquid heat, but I hesitated.

Allowing him to initiate meant he was in control. The thought didn't sit well in my stomach. "I-I want you to, but I'm afraid to give you that power over me."

"Then don't." He peered at me with those beautiful, blue eyes I wanted to sink into. "You've...uh...made amazing progress in the last fifteen minutes."

A nervous giggle erupted from me, and he chuckled along.

"Let's get cleaned up and just hang out for a while, okay?"

Nodding, I moved back and released my hold on his softened cock. The loss of his warmth sent a shiver through me.

I liked being close to him.

A whole hell of a lot more than was probably smart.

Chapter 13

Micah

I didn't want to make any mistakes with Jasmine, but not touching her had me teetering on the edge of insanity. Sure, I got off, but I longed to make her feel good too. To please her and bring her pleasure she'd never experienced before. If given the chance to show her what a loving touch could be, I felt sure healing would happen faster.

But like I'd told her, she'd made amazing progress. I wasn't about to fuck that up.

Jasmine sat in the middle of the couch, and I settled in one corner, laying my arm over the back without touching her. She scooted closer, almost brushing against my side.

"I think I have a new favorite pastime," she murmured, staring at my lips.

I smirked. "You're welcome to kiss me whenever."

"Off the clock," she tacked on with a hint of question in her voice.

"As long as we're in agreement, then I have zero issues of you taking whatever you want, whenever you want it."

"This?" She lifted her gaze to my eyes.

I opened my mouth but shut it again, wondering how the hell to put into words what I felt for her. Lust? Protectiveness? Friendship didn't begin to put a dent in the truth of our connection. I wondered if she experienced the same, or if I was simply a guy she found attractive enough to test herself with. Once able to move on, would I even be a part of her future? That thought twisted my stomach into knots. I did not want to even consider another man laying his hands on her even with her consent.

"Well, what I'm feeling for you is much more than mere friendliness," I finally said. "I care about you. I'd like to see you healed completely and live unhindered. I also want to be a part of that life."

Her brows shot up, and her head tilted to the side.

God, did I want to kiss her.

"But," I continued before she could speak, "if you're using me just to test yourself, I'm available for that too. Your needs are more important to me than my own." *Fuck*, did that hurt to say.

Her lips parted, and I filled my lungs with her sweetness as she moved in toward me. Already given the green light on kissing, I responded once she made first contact.

Jasmine had told me in detail what the foster asshole had done to her, and I had no desire to remind her of his touch, including anything that might feel like force. I wanted to devour her mouth, take everything she offered, but contented myself with gentleness. Lips brushing, tongues tasting in a slow, languid dance made my cock swell to life.

She leaned in closer, her soft breasts pressing against me, her hand on my chest. Both of us breathed heavy when she finally pulled back.

"I really want you to try touching me," she whispered.

I didn't need a second offering. Slowly, I placed my palm over the back of the hand she still held to my chest.

She didn't shy away but simply stared up at me as I laced my fingers through hers.

"You trust me?" I asked.

"Yes."

"Do you know what a safeword is?"

She nodded. "I...um. Well, I've studied the BDSM lifestyle over the previous couple of months. I'm definitely intrigued by it." She shrugged, her face a gorgeous shade of pink.

Fucking hell, this woman.

"We'll go with red," I rasped. "Yellow is you're not sure and want a break, and green means you're good to try for more."

"Alright." She still sounded too hesitant for me to make a move in good conscience.

"If you've read up on BDSM," I said, "then you know you hold all the power, Jasmine. You're in charge of what you do and don't want. You might believe allowing me to touch you is me having the upper hand—but I will obey whatever you say, understand?"

Her body went pliant, a steady exhale sagging her shoulders. "I-I hadn't thought of it like that."

"You're in control. Always."

She swallowed and nodded, tears hazing her eyes. "Thank you."

"No need to thank me. These are the rules I chose to live by as a Dom. My code of conduct, and no matter how much I want to ravish every inch of your skin, I'm not going to push for more than you're willing to allow."

Her smile slid over me like warm sunshine.

I stood and pulled her to her feet. She kept her hand in mine as I led her across the living room toward my bedroom.

The asshole foster kid had gone into her room late at night. She'd told me that memories of his looming over her with his harsh grip and crowding her with his dick brought on panic attacks. She still slept with a bright night-light.

Her steps slowed as we entered my bedroom, but I pushed the dimmer up to full brilliance, lighting every corner of the room. She eyed the bed and lifted her gaze to me, once more unsure.

"We're going to snuggle," I said. "Face to face."

Shoulders relaxing, she smiled, her pale green eyes losing their hesitancy. "I haven't cuddled since I was a little girl on my mom's lap."

"Come on." I let go of her hand, kicked off my shoes, and lay down on my side in the middle of the bed fully clothed. No looming, no planking over her lush body, no dominant words or actions...just good old fashioned spooning—or as close as she was willing to get.

She slipped out of her flip-flops and climbed up beside me, keeping a foot or so of space between us, tucking both of her hands beneath a pillow. A lock of blonde hair slid down over her cheek.

I moved slowly, my fingertip brushing her ear while tucking the hair behind it.

Her chest swelled, breath held.

"Jasmine?" I checked in, keeping the tip of my fingers on her hair.

Eyes wide, she stared at me.

I waited.

Her breaths came in pants, and I wasn't sure if it was due to anxiety or desire.

"Want me to stop?" I whispered, still unmoving.

"N-No...not yet."

I trailed my fingertips over her ear, watching her eyes the entire time. "Color?"

"I'm okay—green."

"Just like in your dream," I murmured, "but you tell me when you've had enough."

Humming an agreement, she nodded.

Avoiding her wrist since Billy had seemed fond of restraining her there, I started at her forearm. A gentle caresses upward led me to the crook of her bent elbow to her shoulder.

Jasmine shivered but didn't safeword.

I traced around her collarbone, lingering as she had done when showing me what she imagined. "Okay?"

"Mmm," she hummed, although her breaths still came in pants, wariness in her eyes.

She trusted me to touch her—I had to trust her ability to say red when she reached her limit.

I crept my fingers up her neck toward her ear and down her jawline. I brushed my thumb over her parted lips.

Black pupils dominated the green of her eyes. No fear or anxiety shone from her gaze as she stared at me, just hesitant need.

My cock throbbed, but I held onto my self-control, trailing my fingers back down her neck and feathering over the swell of her breasts atop her shirt. She shivered and slid her upper arm to drape over her hip, giving me access to her chest. Her nipples hardened beneath the tank top.

"Can I touch you there?" I asked, wanting verbal consent.

"Yes," she whispered, her voice breathless with desire.

I rubbed my thumb over first one then the other nipple.

Her breath hitched, but she didn't shy away.

"Okay, little lamb?" I asked again, the pet name spilling off my lips without thought. I liked it. A lot.

Lower lip between her teeth, she nodded. "Please don't stop."

She had told me that I didn't touch her gently in her dreams, but I wasn't about to fuck up the chance to feel her soft skin beneath my hands by getting rough and causing pain.

I toyed with the hem of her tank top for a few seconds without breaking our stare.

"Yes," she whispered.

She shivered again as my fingertips caressed her bare stomach. I inched my way up her torso, and she shifted, allowing me to stretch her shirt up and over her bra-covered breasts. Sliding my fingers over the tops of her satiny-soft swells parted her lips again. The pulse in her neck jumped.

"Color?"

I expected yellow with how she watched me.

"Green."

My dick bucked, but I ignored the throb in my balls and slid a thumb beneath her bra cup to brush my pad over her hard nipple.

"Oh..." She closed her eyes, and her body took over, arching into my touch. "More. P-Please."

Although I wanted to sit up and yank her top off, feasting first my eyes then my mouth on her pert tits, I gently tugged her shirt higher. Jasmine wiggled, swore, and pulled it off overhead with an abrupt movement that made me have to bite back a smile.

My stomach fluttered like I was some nervous kid, not a thirty-six-year-old man with hundreds of sexual experiences under my belt.

White cotton held her breasts high and plump. My

fucking mouth watered, my gaze glued to the dark pink of her nipples showing through the material.

I trailed my fingertips over the tops again, down her cleavage, feathering across one tight nub.

She moaned and licked her lips.

"You're in control, Jasmine," I murmured, my heart pounding. "Tell me what you need."

"I-I want your mouth on me."

Fuuuuuck.

Slithering like a ninja, I slid down a good two feet, putting my face in line with her chest. Still lying on my side, I lifted her bra above her tits, freeing them.

Large nipples, pink and contracted, begged for my lips. My tongue and teeth.

I palmed a breast and leaned in, breathing in the sweet scent of her skin. Brushing my lips over her furled nub arched her into me again, and I closed my lips over one.

"Oh, God," she groaned, threading her fingers in my hair and holding me tight against her in a green light if ever there was one.

My dick throbbed in my jeans, but keeping my touch soft, I drove us both fucking insane, suckling, gently nibbling. Jasmine gasped and moaned, pressing the length of her body along mine. Her hips moved against me with instinctive need, the actions as hungry and desperate as the noises coming from her mouth.

"So much for just snuggling," I murmured around her flesh.

She giggled with what sounded like nervous energy. "I-I can't seem to help myself around you. Sorry?"

"Don't be." I lathed over her nipple. "I honestly didn't have any intention of taking things this far when I brought you in here."

"It's okay—I like this. A hell of a lot."

Cursing, I suckled a bit harder.

Jasmine moaned and clutched me closer. I should have known she would push herself—and me to a breaking point.

But she dealt the cards, and I wouldn't fold until she told me to.

I touched her knee and slowly inched my fingers upward to the hem of her skirt and down again to the back of her knee. A slight tug, and she lifted her leg, her thigh resting over my waist, her skirt riding upward.

Kissing along her breasts and neck, I slid my hand between us, my fingertips feathering over the lace of her soaked panties.

"Color, Jasmine?" I murmured against the side of her warm breast while gently rubbing her distended clit through cotton.

"So green," she moaned, making my cock jerk inside its prison. "Green—*bright* green, Sir."

"Fuck." She couldn't talk like that... I groaned and suckled on her nipple again, doing exactly how she'd shown me. Fingertip along the edge of her panties, slip beneath, up over her soaked slit to her clit.

The asshole had rutted harshly against her while shoving his fingers inside of her, so I kept my touch high inside her damp curls, drawing wet circles around her clit as she pulled on my hair.

"Please, Micah." She panted for breath, her chest heaving in my face as her hips gyrated, seeking release. "I-I need more."

"I don't want to hurt you," I murmured and flicked my tongue over her tight nipple.

"Put your fingers inside me."

Well, fuck. She didn't need to tell me twice. I slid a

single finger over her slit, rimming the quivering hole of her pussy. A graze of my teeth over her pebbled nipple earned me a curse.

"Please…" She thrust against my hand, and I pressed an inch into her tight sheath before pulling back out. "Don't stop. *Please*, Micah."

Hot and slick, her pussy clenched on my finger as I pushed in again, and she wrapped her lower leg around my hip, her hands grasping at my head and hair.

Jasmine's pussy was so. Fucking. Tight. *Goddamnit*. I clenched my eyes shut and grabbed my balls with my free hand, tugging them down the best I could through my jeans. I was going to nut like a kid. Fucking hell…the noises on her lips, how she writhed against me as I slow-fucked her with a single finger made me fucking insane.

I rubbed my thumb over her clit, and she convulsed, nails digging into my scalp. "Micah! O-Oh!"

Up to my third knuckle, I felt her pussy spasm with wet heat. I gritted my teeth and continued to fuck into her warmth, giving Jasmine what she cried out for while climaxing on my finger.

Once she quieted and went limp, chest heaving, I slipped my touch from between her thighs and lifted my hand to my face. Her creamy cum smeared over me.

Sated green eyes peered down at me, and I held her gaze, flicking out my tongue up one side of my middle finger and down the other, tasting her musky sweetness.

A deep noise rumbled in my chest as her tang coated my mouth and made me lust for more. "You taste so fucking good, Jasmine."

She swallowed audibly and stared at me as I sucked my finger clean.

My balls ached like a motherfucker, and my cock dug

into the zipper. I ninja-slid back up so our heads lay on the same pillow. I placed my hand on my hip, above where her knee still rested on me. "As good as your dreams?"

She laughed without a trace of nervousness. "A thousand times better." A deep sigh pressed her chest against me, and she brushed her lips over mine. "My new favorite pastime," she murmured, pulling back and settling her gaze on my eyes again.

A smirk lifted the corner of my lips. "Like I said, I'm always available."

She smiled and ran her fingers along my jaw. "I think I might be addicted to you, Micah Fox."

"I'm a good addiction to have." I wasn't able to keep arrogance from my tone.

A giggle puffed her breath across my lips, and unable to help myself, I leaned in to kiss her. Slow and gentle when I wanted to devour.

We'll get there, I told myself a few minutes later as she actually snuggled against me, her face in my neck and hand finding mine atop my hip.

Fucking heaven on earth.

Chapter 14

Jasmine

The damn hairs on the back of my neck stood on end when I got home. I scanned the seemingly quiet neighborhood before unlocking my car and climbing out into the dark night. Streetlights cast plenty of shadows to hide behind, but I didn't see anything suspicious.

My heart thumped as I hurried inside the house, locking up behind me. The youngest of three girls and the only one still living at home, I ended up alone a lot on Friday nights, Mom and Dad's date night.

I grabbed a glass of water, went upstairs to my room, and texted Dina.

Me: **I know you don't think I should get involved with Micah, but he's the most decent man I've ever met.**

The phone rang just like I'd expected.

"Got something more to tell me?" Dina said instead of a greeting.

"Maybe."

She sighed. "Please just be careful," she said, sounding resigned. "I'd hate for you to have another breakdown."

"I'm not going to." I flopped on my bed and smiled at the ceiling. "I touched him, Dina. He sat still as a stone, holding to his promise not to put his hands on me unless I asked him to." Butterflies fluttered in my stomach. "His shoulders are so broad. His hair is silky soft," I murmured, remembering the heat of him on my fingertips.

"*Did* you ask him to touch you?"

I hesitated a few seconds, but Dina was my big sister, the only other confidant besides Liz who was busy with her own life and Mom who would insist on going a hell of a lot slower than Micah and I had done.

"I kissed him." Dina didn't say a word, and I hurried on. "I've made huge steps in getting better. I kissed him and didn't feel a trace of anxiety. Not a trace!" I breathed the words, a wide smile on my lips. "He hasn't taken advantage of my forwardness, either. I'll be careful, I promise, but I'm not stopping."

"Jaz—"

"No. I'm going forward if he's willing, as far as I can test my limits. I want to be able to hold Aaron's brother's arm when we walk down the aisle and dance at your wedding next month. I look forward to enjoying myself in public again like I used to when I was little and didn't fear bumping into people. You don't know what it's like to want to fold in on yourself whenever a man gets too close."

A heavy sigh came over the line. "You're right. I'm sorry. I just can't stand the thought of seeing you get hurt."

"I'll take a broken heart if it means I can touch a guy without losing my shit," I responded immediately.

"Broken hearts suck."

I snorted. "Can't be as bad as what I've been dealing with for over twelve years."

"Again, you're probably right. Love you, Jaz."

My insides settled as I smiled. "Love you, too, Sis."

JB

I woke with a start, my heart pounding as I scrambled to sit.

The night-light I couldn't sleep without shone brightly, allowing me to see into every corner of my bedroom as I jerked my head around, scanning for the face I'd seen in my nightmare.

Hand to my chest, I inhaled while counting. Exhaled through my parted lips.

It's nothing. Just a dream.

I lay back down, still rubbing at my chest and the knot of anxiety threatening to expand and squeeze the air from my lungs.

I hadn't dreamed about the asshole in over a year. What had brought the shit back to my subconscious that I would remember the feel of him grinding his hardness against my body every chance he'd gotten?

My stomach churned, and I clenched my eyes, willing the memories away.

I forced my mind on Micah, my new favorite place. His delicious lips and sweet breath. Gentle touch on my heated skin. My racing heart slowed a bit, but the thoughts of my boss kept it at a steady pace, erasing the unease over what I'd seen while sleeping.

What would come next for him and I?

I planned on touching Micah whenever possible throughout the day and not just in sexual ways. I needed to know if the arousal he brought to life in my body trumped my issue, or if nonsexual touch with him would be just as comfortable and addictive.

The zap of energy I felt every time our skin brushed acted as though it blasted all insecurity issues right out the door.

I needed to test myself outside of Micah, I realized, rolling over and weaseling an arm under my pillow. The thought of coming into contact with another man, however, tightened the vise around my chest I was all too familiar with.

I'll start with the easiest person available, I thought, closing my eyes. Small steps forward were better than none, and the sooner I learned how to continue on with my progress, the sooner I could fulfill all the fantasies I'd been dreaming up for what seemed like forever.

ℍ

The next morning, I went downstairs to find Mom and Dad drinking their coffee and watching NECN like they did every Saturday morning.

I ambled toward the kitchen and coffeepot, intent on grabbing a mug. My hand shook while pouring.

Mere nerves, I told myself.

"Pull up your big girl panties and just do it," I muttered to myself.

I returned to the living room and paused by Dad's chair. His thinning gray hair stood up, and I reached out a hand to smooth it down. He was the man I should trust the most but hadn't touched in twelve years.

His body tensed.

"Morning, Daddy," I whispered, my eyes stinging.

A sob caught in Mom's throat, and I glanced over at her,

my hand still resting on top of Dad's warm head. My throat tightened. She stared at me wide-eyed, fingertips to her lips.

Dad stirred beneath my touch, and I removed my hand, turning my focus back on him.

Dark, wide eyes stared up at me, brimming with unshed tears.

"One step at a time," I told him as wetness slid down my cheeks. "I'm going to beat this."

His Adam's apple bobbed as he swallowed. "You are, pumpkin. I'm so damn proud of you."

A dozen or so tears fell between the three of us, and I ended up sitting beside Dad, his warm, calloused hand wrapped around mine, my head on his shoulder. The lingering scent of his aftershave I hadn't sniffed in far too long swarmed over me, bringing the comfort it always used to when I'd been an innocent child.

An hour or so later, I went back upstairs, my heart a million times lighter. I couldn't stop smiling at the hope in my chest and, on a whim, grabbed my phone to text Micah.

Me: **I held my daddy's hand today for the first time in twelve years.**

I chewed on the inside of my lip while waiting. The ding made me squeak.

Micah: **I'm so proud of you!**

Heart speeding and giggling, I texted as fast as my fingers could move. **I wouldn't have ever come this far without you. Thank you!!**

Micah: **Like I said, I'm always available.**

I wanted to ask if he wanted company right then but chickened out. While contemplating what to text, another ding came through.

Micah: **What are you up to today? It's a**

perfect day for sitting by the ocean and digging toes in the sand.

More uninhibited laughter from my lips reminded me of when I'd been a young tween, twittering and whispering about boys with my friends. Friends I'd lost after the shit happened because I couldn't bear being around people.

I love the beach, I texted back.

Micah: **I'll come pick you up around eleven?**

I wanted to send heart emojis and kissy faces but settled for a simple thumbs-up.

It figured I would cut myself shaving, but that was what I got for rushing. I had an hour to get ready, but the nervousness kept tremors shuddering through my body, making preciseness a joke. I opted for a few swipes of waterproof mascara, and that was it. Had I attempted more, I probably would have ended up in the ER with an eyeliner pencil somehow jammed into my eye.

I stood by the window, chewing on a fingernail, my heart jumping—no vise squeezing. "He's here!" I squealed, turning around.

Both of my parents had gotten up and ready for the day but had returned to their favorite spots in the living room for a day of relaxing and doing nothing—their usual Saturday routine.

"Do we get to meet him?" Dad asked, standing and setting aside the paper he'd been reading.

"I'd love you to," I said, hurrying to the door.

Micah's gaze flitted down over my see-through cover-up thrown over the olive green bikini I wore. His brows rose as his gaze met mine, but he straightened and smiled, holding out his hand.

Dad, I noted, suddenly realizing he'd come up behind

me. "Micah," I said and cleared my throat and moved to the side, "this is my dad, Frank."

"Mr. Swift." Micah stepped up onto the stoop's top step and shook Daddy's hand.

"Mr. Fox, come on in."

I moved back and shut the door behind Micah. Dad wasn't a small man at six foot, but Micah towered over him by a good three inches, making the entryway seem stiflingly small. I found myself leaning toward Micah, wanting to touch rather than shying away as I would have done a month ago.

"My wife, Marsha," Daddy said as Mom moved toward us.

Appreciation for his virility and hot looks lit in Mom's eyes. She might be in her early sixties, but she wasn't dead yet. "Nice to finally meet you, Mr. Fox."

"Same to you," Micah replied, shaking her hand.

"Dina always spoke so highly of you," Mom said.

"Past tense?" Micah asked, glancing down at me with a smirk.

Mom's light laughter tinkled in the tiny area. "She claims you're an honorable man, which is why she encouraged Jasmine to work for you."

Micah turned back toward my parents, and my feet itched to get going before I grew embarrassed or antsy from the lies both Dina and I had told our conservative parents. At least Micah knew we'd kept the truth about his business from them and wouldn't open his mouth and insert his foot.

"You have hardworking, lovely daughters," Micah claimed, sending warmth through my chest. "I've been blessed to have them both in the office. I hope I never have to hire anyone else, because I'll never be able to fill Jasmine's shoes."

I damn near swooned to the floor while Dad beamed, and Mom's face glowed.

"So!" I grabbed my beach bag from where I'd set it by the front door. "Ready to go?" I couldn't get out to the car fast enough—I knew that glint in my mom's eyes and wasn't about to give her the opportunity to invite Micah for dinner.

I wanted him all to myself.

I settled back in the air-conditioned car and clicked my seatbelt as Micah shut my door and made his way around the front. Movement in my periphery pulled my attention to the neighbor's house. An overweight man hurried around the corner and out of sight into the backyard. He wasn't Mr. Donovan, our neighbor.

I rubbed goose bumps from my arm and turned back around as Micah slid into the driver's seat.

"Ready for some sun and sand?" he asked, hitting the ignition button.

I'm ready for much more than that. I bit my tongue, capturing my runaway mouth just in time from embarrassing me. "Absolutely," I said instead. "Then pizza and ice cream, and a final long walk on the beach as the sun sets."

Micah chuckled and pulled away from the curb. "No room for spontaneity?"

"I'm game for pretty much anything." A definite hint toward the physical laced my voice.

"Anything?" His smirk and sideways glance warmed my face and settled heat between my thighs.

"Anything." I sounded breathless as a needy whore, but I didn't give a shit. I wanted Micah Fox and his thick, long cock inside me. I squeezed my thighs together, praying to God I didn't leave a wet spot on his seat.

"Mmm," his voice rumbled, worsening my aroused state. "I like the way you're thinking, but I refuse to rush this and cause a backslide. You're doing so well—too fast in all honesty, although my body disagrees with my better sense."

My smile faded as disappointment swept over me like a cold wave of salty ocean water.

"We've been heading on a crash course toward what we both desire," Micah continued, glancing over at me, "but I have zero wish to fuck it up, Jasmine."

"If it's what we both want, how could fucking fuck it up?"

He groaned. "That mouth of yours..."

"Well?"

Lips in a thin line, he exhaled slowly while pulling onto the highway. "I'm afraid."

I stared at his profile and clenched my hands on my lap to keep from running my fingers over his silky soft hair and scruffy jaw. "Of all the men in the world, I'd think you're the last one who would be afraid of fucking."

"I don't want to dredge up memories." He glanced my way for a brief second, his gaze warm yet full of wariness. "I fear pushing you back to where you were three months ago, talking yourself out of a panic attack because of shaking a man's hand."

"When I think of being with you, Micah," I said, my voice a mere whisper from adrenaline and nervousness rushing through me, "I don't experience any signs of anxiety. The vise that used to clamp my lungs whenever someone got too close isn't anywhere to be found. My heart races, and I fight for breath like I am right now because I'm so turned on, and I can't think of anything else." I swallowed hard at his low curse. "But it's not just the thought of sex," I rushed on. "I touched my father today for the first time in twelve years, Micah. No anxiety. No tightness in my chest. The steps I've made in the past couple of months aren't just about wanting your dick."

His chest lifted and shuddered back into place. "I'm glad to hear that." He glanced over at me and smiled with a pained grimace as though his balls ached. "So maybe after that long walk on the beach, we can head back to my place for a late dinner?"

My pussy clenched tight. "And dessert."

He chuckled and adjusted the swelled bulge inside his swimming trunks. "I'm finding it very difficult to say no to you."

"Good." I grinned and faced forward again, not one trace of painful nervousness skittering over my skin. That feeling making me feel alive? It was desire like I'd experienced the night before in the safety of Micah's bed.

Chapter 15

Micah

Lying on the beach beside Jasmine in that damn bikini...fuck, did I fight my cock's need to swell and thrust deep into her warmth. Jerking off a few minutes before leaving my house to pick her up hadn't helped my libido one fucking bit. The thought of what the night might hold—if everything progressed smoothly—had my entire body aching with desperate yearning.

We moved quickly. Way too fucking fast for safety.

But I had to trust Jasmine to know her limits. We'd discussed the BDSM lifestyle late into the night, and she was well aware of what she was talking about. She'd done her research. Even joined a forum to get her questions answered before the lines of such communication had even opened up between us.

As the sun beat down on us, I asked about her childhood with having two sisters to keep my mind occupied on something other than bringing us both to a state of satiated bliss.

She in turn questioned about mine with my pain-in-the-ass brother. We'd grown up in meager households with kind parents and somewhat decent siblings. While both of our parents had stayed together when most of our friends' hadn't, Jasmine's memories were a bit more pleasant when it came to home life.

My parents had bickered a lot, and it had only gotten worse as they'd grown older. Dad had worked in a machine shop for years, so his hearing wasn't the greatest. Add in his liver issues, and he was sometimes a bastard. I shared a story of what the typical night at their dinner table entailed: one misunderstanding after another that heated until they both raised their voices, neither being heard.

Jasmine giggled, jiggling her breasts I wanted to stripe with my cum. "I'm sorry. It probably isn't funny."

I grumbled and rolled onto my stomach since my cock enjoyed the way her breasts swayed a bit too much. "That's why I don't go home very often. The bickering is worse than nails on a chalkboard. It's bad enough having them over once a month for dinner, but they're the only parents I'll ever have. I've seen too many friends bury theirs and have made an effort to be grateful for their lingering presence in my life."

"You're a good man, Micah," Jasmine stated on a sigh.

I wanted to snort at her statement but didn't. Let the young woman think what she would. Maybe someday, if I got lucky, I would be able to prove her thoughts were in error. I was a sadist through and through. Not many would see that as *good*.

Or perhaps she would appreciate my kinky streak...

"I'm hot."

I propped up on my elbows and ran my gaze slowly down over her oiled-up body. "You are."

Her cheeks flushed, and she pulled her sunglasses off while sitting. "Let's go cool off."

"I'd rather get even more hot and sweaty," I stated while waggling my eyebrows.

She narrowed her gaze while she peered over at me. "Thought you didn't want to rush?"

"Wanting and wishing are two *totally* separate things."

"Are they?" She stood and held out her hand.

My cock twitched but stayed nonthreatening beneath my shorts. I pushed up and laced my fingers through hers, keeping an eye on her face.

She beamed up at me. "See? Nonsexual touch, and I'm still fine."

"Oh, it could be sexual," I murmured, skimming my thumb along the back of her hand, letting her see what I wished for in my steady gaze.

Her breath caught and eyes widened. Those black pupils of hers dilated too.

"Come on," I said, tugging her down the beach between the other people lounging and lying beneath the hot sun. "I really need to cool off."

We stood side by side in the ocean, waist-high in the water as waves swelled, breaking behind us on the beach.

The sun beat down on my head, and I dove through the next wave to wash off the sheen of sweat on my forehead. I came up to find Jasmine had done the same, standing alongside me in water up to her chest. She might look like a drowned rat to some with her blonde hair a bit darker and plastered to her head, but I'd never seen anything so damn fine in my life.

"What?" she asked, pushing her wet hair back from her face.

"You're beautiful."

She smiled, and I reached for her, sliding my hand

down her arm to her hand beneath the water and tugging her toward me.

"Okay?" I asked, drawing her nearer.

"Yes." She closed the distance between us, the heat of her lush body and the cool of the ocean doing a number on my senses.

"Fuck, you feel so good," I murmured, lightly wrapping my arms around her waist as my cock swelled.

She pressed flush against me and wiggled her hips. "So do you."

I growled but kept my touch light against her lower back. "You do that, and I'm not going to be able to walk out of this water without giving everyone a show."

"Mmm." She rubbed her belly against my cock and lifted with the next wave to wrap her legs around my waist.

"Jesus, Jasmine." I swallowed hard, my hands itching to grasp her ass.

A wave rolled by, lifting her breasts as we stared at each other.

"We could do it right here, and no one would know," she whispered, her pupils blown and pulse throbbing in her neck.

"Your first time isn't going to be a rushed, bikini-pulled-to-the-side fuck in the ocean."

Jasmine shuddered in my arms. "God, that sounds divine."

The muscle in my jaw jumped as I fought for control. "And you're so fucking tempting I don't want to say no."

Her light laughter hinted at nervousness, and I pulled my goddamn brain back to solid ground, shifting her sway from my body, hands on her waist. "How about that ice cream?" I asked, settling her onto her feet beneath the water.

She sighed. "Fine."

I let go of her and dove into a couple more cold waves to shrivel my balls.

JE

Fucking torture.

There were no better words to describe being with Jasmine in her flimsy, see-through cover-up and knowing I might actually get a real taste of what lay beneath before night's end. And the way she licked her ice cream cone? I'd been unaware of what need actually was before Jasmine had crashed into my life.

She would eventually be mine, and I couldn't fucking wait, but I wondered about the future of our relationship. A Dom through and through, I got off on having a submissive under me. I enjoyed dishing out pain to bring pleasure.

And even though Jasmine definitely seemed interested in the lifestyle, I highly doubted she would ever be up for that. With her past, I expected there would be no marking her with my hand, let alone a wooden paddle or cane I brought out on rare occasions to prove I held onto my self-control, unlike Dean.

If compatibility proved to be an issue with Jasmine, would an attempted relationship work? The thought hung heavy on my shoulders, but I told myself to take shit one step at a time—just as she'd been doing to distance herself from her past and touch issues. She just happened to move at one hell of a fast pace I wasn't sure I trusted.

But fuck did I want to.

We ambled back down to the beach after finishing our ice cream. I'd had just about enough of the heat, but Jasmine had suggested that sunset walk after I'd picked her up. I could handle another couple of hours until sunset since it meant having her beside me.

I started to sit in the beach chair we'd left in the sand, but she stood, hands on hips, scowling at her spread out towel someone had kicked sand across.

"I think I've had about enough of the sun and sand for today." She glanced at me, her frown relaxing. "Want to take off?"

I hopped back up like a fire lit under my ass. "Let's go."

A few minutes later, we climbed into my car, and I rolled the windows down to let the heat escape a bit before turning on the AC. "Where to?" I asked, pulling out into traffic.

She smiled and shrugged, but I caught the wariness in her eyes.

"We can grab some food and head to my place if you want. Watch a movie. Hang out."

Her laughter also betrayed her nervousness. "Don't feel like cooking?"

"It's too fucking hot," I said, cranking on the AC and putting the windows up.

"Hanging out sounds good." Jasmine's phone rang, and she fished it out of her bag. "Hey, Mom." She listened as her mother's murmuring reached my ears. I couldn't make out the words—and wasn't the type to try.

"Oh."

The word sounded forced, drawing my gaze off the road for a second. Face pale, Jasmine stared out the windshield.

"W-when?" she asked.

A few seconds passed, and I clutched the steering wheel. Obviously, the call had brought bad news.

"I might have seen him this morning, but I got distracted." Her swallow sounded loud over the blasting AC. "Going into Mr. Donovan's backyard."

I frowned at the tremor in her voice.

She blew a deep breath out between her lips. "Okay, I will."

I glanced over at her again to find her peering at me. "I'm sure it'll be all right, Mom, but I'll ask him."

"What's going on?" I asked the second she hung up.

"The asshole is out of jail and moved back."

"I thought he couldn't be anywhere near you," I said, my brow furrowed into a scowl.

"I guess the other side of town is far enough away he isn't breaking the restraining order, but knowing he's close by...I think I saw the back of him when you picked me up." Nerves had gotten the best of her voice, and she all but whispered, her hands clenched around the phone on her lap.

"Fucker," I growled, hold the steering wheel tight as though I wrapped my fingers around his neck. "You should call the cops."

"Just because I thought he was next door doesn't mean shit. A restraining order doesn't do much except get him thrown in jail if he attacks me either."

"Jesus fucking Christ." I felt the need to smash the fuck out of something and wondered if my buddy Cooney had felt the same when Becky's ex had beaten her to the point she landed in the ER.

Zero fucking tolerance.

My blood boiled, and I clung to the steering wheel with white knuckles. "Men like him ought to be disemboweled and shot."

She nodded, and I reached out my hand, hoping like hell a

roadblock hadn't just been thrown in our way. "You okay?" I asked. Without hesitation, she slid her palm against mine, and I squeezed, my insides settling somewhat. "If that fucker comes anywhere near you, I'll feed his balls to him for breakfast."

She laughed, unforced but shaky. "For some strange reason, I believe you."

"What? You don't think I can be a violent person?"

"I...I know you are."

I shot another glance over the console. She peered at me but without fear in her gaze.

"You're referring to the fact I'm a Dom."

"Yes."

"If you know I'm a sadist, why are you with me?" I found myself asking as my anger began to fade.

"I'm not afraid of you."

"Maybe you should be," I said, my voice deadpan, my chest heavy.

"No. You wouldn't ever hurt me." I opened my mouth, but she hurried on. "You wouldn't lay a hand on me to *hurt*, hurt me. Your pain is meant to give pleasure."

My shoulders relaxed, and I settled back in my seat, reminding myself she'd been studying my particular kink. "That's exactly right."

"I don't know if I could be the type of submissive you need though," she whispered a few seconds later. "But I'd like to try things. See what I enjoy and what I don't."

I rubbed my thumb over her hand, unable to speak at her graciousness. Her innocent desire to find middle ground with me.

"Would you be willing to show me...after you, we..." Cheeks pink, she bit on her lower lip.

"I would love to." I lifted our clasped hands and

brushed my lips over her knuckles. "But first, we have a few hurdles to overcome together."

"I'm ready to jump whenever you are." Her breathless voice kicked lust to high gear in my groin.

"So." I released her hand and clutched the steering wheel once more, needing to focus on anything other than hearing and feeling her come around my cock. "What's the plan for dealing with Billy the asshole?"

"My parents wondered if you could take me over to Dina's for the night. Since I thought I saw him, they don't want me home for a couple of days."

"The fucker should have done more time for putting that scar on your neck." I clenched my jaw to keep from cursing until hoarse. "You're not going to Dina's. You're staying with me."

Jasmine didn't reply, and I eventually glanced over at her. Eyes wide, she stared at me.

"Will your parents be all right with that?" I asked.

"I-I honestly don't know."

"Dial your mom. I want to talk to her."

She complied and handed me the phone. It rang twice.

"Hey, pumpkin," her mom's voice sounded in my ear.

"Mrs. Swift, it's Micah Fox."

"Oh!" Her tone betrayed her smile. "Frank and I were just talking about you."

"I wondered why my ears were ringing," I said with a smile, glancing over at Jasmine.

Her lips twitched, her hands once more clasped in her lap.

"I know you asked Jasmine to go to Dina's tonight, but she's going to stay with me." I didn't ask, simply made a statement. "I won't be able to rest tonight without knowing personally she slept safe and sound."

"Oh. Well." She sounded flustered. "I-I suppose that would be okay—if you have a guest room?"

"Of course." That didn't mean Jasmine would be crawling between those sheets though.

"Can I speak with her?"

I handed the phone to Jasmine and returned to clutching the wheel.

"Hey, Mom."

I strained to make out her mom's words but couldn't.

"I will. Yes. *Yes, Mom.*" I caught Jasmine's eye roll. "He's been nothing but a perfect gentleman, and Dina trusts him too." Her cheeks blushed as she cast a sideways glance my way. "I promise. Yes. Love you too, Mom."

Mrs. Swift murmured a bit more.

"I'll call you in the morning." Jasmine hung up and dropped the phone into her bag between her feet.

"The whole 'be careful' talk?" I asked, brow raised as I glanced over at her.

She giggled, lightening my mood. "Yep."

With the news her attacker had moved back into town, I expected the plans for exploring more physical touch that evening had been shot to shit. But I could deal. I didn't want to get involved sexually unless her mind was one hundred percent in, no distraction, no issue to take away or hinder what the experience could be for us.

Jasmine touched my arm.

I loosened my hold on the steering wheel and wrapped my hand around hers once more.

At least she'd reached out to me for comfort. I heaved a deep breath and focused on getting us home where I could lock us in, set the alarm system, and relax the best my aching balls allowed.

Chapter 16

Jasmine

"**G**lass of wine?" Micah asked, shutting the garage door behind me as we stepped into his kitchen.

"That would be great, thanks."

He keyed in the code for the alarm, tossed his keys on the island, and took two wine glasses from the cabinet. "Red or white?"

"Red." I shrugged as he glanced at me. "Gets me loopier faster than white."

"A little escaping reality might be a good idea," he agreed.

Heaving a huge sigh, I lounged on the couch, eyes closed, head tipped back. Billy had gotten out of jail—and stalked me regardless of the restraining order. Unfortunately, a simple slip of paper hardly ever hindered a wacko from shadowing or going after their obsession.

A sense of discomfort had assailed me the second Mom told me the news, but I didn't experience fear like I should have. Perhaps taking back some of my confidence had strengthened me to stand up to the threat of him. Or maybe, being with Micah gave me more comfort than I'd thought possible.

"Here."

I lifted my head and took the glass of red from Micah, our fingers brushing as he released his hold. Zero anxiety coursed through me. The knot that had twisted my stomach when Mom called unraveled a little bit more, and I withered in my seat.

Micah settled beside me. He held up his drink. "To assholes getting what they deserve and to moving on with your life."

"I'll cheers to that," I said with a light laugh, clinking my glass to his. "I'm so ready for both."

We sipped, and he lowered his gaze to the stem wrapped by his fingers. "I think we ought to forget those plans for dessert tonight."

My heart plummeted. "What? Why?"

He shrugged and glanced up at me. A furrow etched his brow. "If and when we take the next step in this growing thing between us, your whole head needs to be in the game. I don't want anything tickling at the back of your skull, something that would take away from the experience or keep you from enjoying yourself to the fullest."

I thought of being *full*—stuffed with Micah's cock—and remembered the way his touch down there had turned me on, how quickly he'd made me come. Need lifted my hand, and I swiped my thumb over his lips. "When you touch me, I can't think of anything else. I'm consumed by you and what you're doing to me. Honestly, I forgot my name when you made me come the other night."

His low groan lit a fire between my thighs. "Do you know how hard it is to be honorable and keep my focus straight when you say things like that?"

"I want you, Micah. Forget the wine. Forget reality. Forget everything but you and me. Kissing. Touching. Please."

Heat filled his gaze, sending twinges through my pussy. He placed his glass on the coffee table and took mine, doing the same. "If at any time I make you uncomfortable, you know what to say."

I nodded firmly. "Stop or red."

"I'll honor—*obey*—both, no matter how or when you state either word." Micah stood and held out his hand.

Fully trusting him, I pressed my palm against his. He tugged me to my feet, sliding his other hand along my cheek. "I'm going to make this good for you, Jasmine. A night you'll never forget." His lips closed over mine, and I clung to his shirt as my knees threatened to buckle beneath me.

He snaked an arm around my back, holding me loosely —too far away from his hard body and the heat emanating from him.

Pressing my chest to his brought a groan to his lips, and his arm banded tighter.

This. This is what I've been missing.

Closeness outside hurried humping. Connection.

Beyond the physical.

How had I lived without touch outside of my mother, sisters, and nephews for so long? Micah's hold was heaven, his lips the sweetest escape on earth, and his tongue... *God*, his tongue.

He pulled back too soon, leaving me weak-kneed and trembling. Without a word, he took my hand and led me to the bedroom. The sight of his massive bed sent a shiver down my spine, pebbling my skin but in a good way.

I recalled our so-called snuggling. Coming on his finger—

"Can I undress you?" he asked, stepping close to my back but not touching me.

"Yes," I whispered, unable to move as his breath caressed my ear.

Gentle hands gathered my cover-up at my hips and slowly lifted the material, pulling it up and over my head. His fingertips brushed my hair over my shoulder and tugged on the bikini tie at the nape of my neck.

"I've been dreaming about taking this off your body all day long," he murmured, fingertips trailing down to the second tie at the middle of my back.

More delicious shivers snaked their way down my entire body, and I bit the inside of my lip to keep from moaning.

He untied the second tie, and my bikini top slipped off my breasts and fell to the floor. My breath sounded loud in my ears atop the thump of my heartbeat.

Micah's fingers slid under the edges of my bikini bottoms at my hips. "Okay?" he murmured in my ear, the heat of his almost-touching body flaming through me.

Swallowing, I nodded, and he tugged, squatting behind me to lift first one of my feet then the other, helping me step from the scrap of material soaked by my arousal.

He groaned. "You smell so fucking good."

I closed my eyes as he breathed deep and ran his nose up through my ass crack.

Holy hell. I gulped.

"So fucking good." Standing, he returned his heat close to my shoulders and neck without touching. "Lay down on the bed, my little lamb."

A low moan escaped me at the possessive in front of the nickname he'd gifted me. I *was* an innocent lamb...but soon to be soiled in the best way possible. I managed to make my legs move, and I sat on the edge of the bed, scooting back to lay down. Tremors rippled through me, but I didn't gasp for breath.

Micah stared between my legs while reaching behind his head to grab his T-shirt and rip it off overhead.

My mouth dried. Even though I'd been checking him out all day on the beach, I couldn't get enough of his physique. Thick pecs, ripples of abs leading down to that luscious V disappearing beneath his shorts, and that hard, tenting ridge...

He reached beneath the waistband and pulled out his cock. "Is this what you want?"

I licked my lower lip, need coursing through my entire body. "Yes," I whispered my answer.

Another groan left him as he pushed his shorts all the way down. He hesitated, his gaze roaming up my legs, to my pussy, up over my breasts, until our eyes finally met, his hand stroking along his length the entire time. "You're sure?"

"I've never wanted anything so damn much in my life."

He kneeled on the bed by my feet and crawled forward, my legs spreading to accommodate him without conscious effort. "Keep your eyes on me," he murmured, his lips brushing over my knee, "so you know who's touching you."

My chest tightened over his concern, different from anxiety's hold. I propped up on my elbows to watch him dip his head to brush his lips over my inner knee...up my thigh.

Our gazes latched as he shifted onto his belly, making himself comfortable between my splayed thighs. Those dark blue eyes of his turned navy, nostrils flaring as he inhaled deeply.

I bit my lower lip to keep from begging him to put his mouth on me.

"I'm going to taste you."

Oh, God. Gulping, I nodded.

He licked a lazy stroke through my soaked lower lips.

"Shit." A tremor rushed over me, and I wanted to throw my head back, eyes closed while basking in a world I'd only dreamed of. Blinking, I forced my eyelids up, drowning in his heated gaze as he licked along my slit again.

A deep groan rumbled through his chest. "So sweet. Need more."

"Take it," I whispered, trembling from intense arousal I didn't know how to handle.

He dove in, suckling and nibbling until my thighs squeezed his head and my hands fisted in his hair.

I panted for breath, whines escaping me, pleadings for more as he took long, languid tastes of the wetness slipping from my pussy. "I need you," I groaned as he suckled my clit deep into his mouth, the slight sting only adding to my arousal. "Please, Micah."

He kissed his way up my stomach, careful to keep his weight off of me. Palmed my breasts and suckled until I writhed beneath him. Open-mouthed kisses swept over my collarbone and back again, and I finally closed my eyes, giving over to the absolute lust wracking my body.

"I'm okay, Micah," I whimpered, trying to reassure him that I was ready, that I wanted him desperately. "Need you so damn much—"

He slid the back of his cock up through my swollen, wet labia, and I grasped at his waist with my thighs, trying to make him take me.

"Condom," he muttered, reaching for the side table.

"I don't want anything between us," I whispered,

opening my eyes again, meeting his heated stare. "I'm on the pill, and I've seen your last test results." I refused to be embarrassed by my snooping. I was Elite's secretary and had unhindered access to everyone's personal folders.

"Jasmine..."

"Please, Micah," I begged, wrapping my ankles around his tight ass. "I want your bare cock inside me. I-I know it might hurt at first, but I trust you to make it feel good. I want it. *You.* Need to feel your touch inside my body without latex to take away from what I've been dreaming about since the moment I set eyes on you."

Cradling my face in his hands, he brushed his lips across mine, gentle and sweet as though cherishing the moment.

Wiggling my hips beneath him got his cock pressed against my entrance, and I moaned a complaint when he continued on with the slow tongue-fucking of my mouth instead of pushing into my willing body.

I whimpered again, and he chuckled.

"Patience, little lamb."

"I'm *dying*! Been waiting so damn long for someone to make me brave enough to offer up my virginity. Thought of this moment for years, then you come along, blow past all my barriers, and I'm burning up inside, needing—"

His ass flexed beneath my ankles, and his cock breached my opening. He stilled about an inch inside me and lifted his head, peering into my eyes as though expecting me to freak the fuck out.

"More," I whispered, lifting my hips, desperate to be filled.

Another two inches sank into me before he paused again.

I dug my fingernails into his back. "Goddammit, Micah! I'm fine! Fucking take me already!"

A growl rumbled from his chest, and he captured my mouth and thrust, bottoming out deep inside my body.

"Oh shit!" I gasped against his mouth over the sting, the stretching fullness—I felt sure I split in two he was so fucking big.

"Fuck. Jesus—I'm so fucking sorry." He started to pull out, but I held him tight with my legs, grasped my hands in his hair, and tugged his mouth to mine.

"I see only you, Micah," I said against his mouth, pulling him toward me with my ankles until he sank back in, the head of him brushing over my cervix. "All I feel is you. It burns but in a good way. It's delicious—*you're* delicious." I bit his lower lip.

"You little minx," he muttered as a shudder rippled down his body. "Fuck, Jasmine, the shit you do to my head."

"Kiss me."

He bruised my mouth with his, pulling out of my pussy and slowly sliding inside me again.

I arched, trying to take him deeper and have him touch me everywhere, but he planked over me, retreated, and angled his hips to push in once more.

"Oh God!" I shoved my breasts up against his chest and grabbed hold of his ass, my nails digging into his skin. "I need you," I gasped. "Touch me—all of me," I begged, near sobbing. "*Please*, Micah."

"Jesus," he hissed, trembling as though keeping himself away from me physically hurt.

"Please," I whispered again.

"Can't fucking deny you. Shit." He groaned and pressed in deep while lowering his weight, his heat atop my chest.

I moaned, wrapping myself around him, holding him close. "Perfect—knew it," I whispered, peering into his navy blues.

"You're mine, Jasmine," he said, brushing my hair away from my face and cradling my cheeks. "Every fucking inch of your body, your mind, is mine. No one else has had you—no one else ever fucking will."

Quite the claim while he was balls deep inside my body, but I felt his words even deeper inside my soul.

"Yes," I whispered since I had zero wish to argue.

He'd spoken truth.

Micah gyrated his hips, grinding his pelvis against my clit, and I gasped, my back attempting to arch beneath him. "I want you to come all over my cock. I need you to squeeze me with this hot pussy. Milk every last drop of cum from my balls that have been aching for you all. Fucking. Day." He thrust with each word.

I moaned my agreement, chasing the high awaiting me while clutching at his rippling muscles.

He palmed my breast and lifted it to his mouth, gently nipping, tongue soothing as his thrusts grew faster. More forceful. His teeth closed over my nipple, and my world blew to the fucking stars.

"Fuck! Micah!" I convulsed beneath him, my hands tangled in his hair and pulling him closer, my thighs squeezing along with every spasm deep inside my pussy sending gushes of cum all over his cock. "Oh God!"

"Fuck, yes." He planked over me, lowering his gaze to where he slammed into me over and over as aftershocks continued to shudder through me. "You're so fucking hot. Fucking perfect."

He slammed in deep and tipped his head back, veins sticking out in his neck, jaw clenched.

Hot spurts erupted against my cervix as he groaned my name. He fell on top of me, claiming my mouth while filling me with his cum.

My body buzzed, hummed with energy. Finally living.

His kisses and thrusts slowed until he relaxed his weight on me and buried his face in my neck. The scruff on his cheeks prickled, and I gasped, shying away.

"Shit!" He pulled back, his still-hard cock slipping from my body.

I giggled and grabbed his arms before he retreated completely. "Just tickled is all. I'm fine. A little...too empty too quickly, but good."

His slow smile warmed me through, settling in my chest as he slid back up my body again, nestling his softening cock against my soaked core. "Sure you're okay?"

"Fan-fucking-tastic." I laughed. "Holy shit, that was awesome."

He grinned. "High praise like that will get you whatever the fuck you want."

I slid my ankles back up around his ass and squeezed. "How about another *fuck* whenever I want?"

"God, yes." He brushed my lips with his, and I gave over to his probing tongue and the warmth rekindling between my thighs.

Chapter 17

Micah

The moonlight poured through the open drapes, lighting Jasmine's sleeping face. Swollen lips parted, cheeks still flushed, she rested, her blonde hair a riotous mess on my pillow. The pulse beat steadily in her neck, and my gaze trailed lower to where the sheet slipped beneath one of her breasts. They were perfect globes that fit in my hand, soft nipples on the tips making my mouth water.

My little lamb...my woman. Every inch of her belonged to me and only me—and she'd agreed when I'd boldly claimed her as such.

She didn't know it yet, but she wasn't going back to her parents' place.

I'd cleaned her up, and she'd fallen asleep with her head on my chest after a solid two hours of cuddles and pillow talk—two things of which I never did. Asshole Billy and the fact he might be stalking her hadn't come up a single time. He lingered in my mind, though. I wouldn't rest easy until he'd been dealt with.

While I wasn't a violent person, I knew a shady character or two. Temptation to send him deep out to sea in pieces teased with my conscience. The knowledge he'd violated her, fucked up her head for so many years, tensed my body. Made me see fucking red.

I wanted to kill the motherfucker.

Jasmine sighed and rolled from me, the sheet slipping low across her back and pulling me into reality again.

Unable to help myself, I feathered my fingertips down her side to the dip of her waist and back up over the flare of her hip, pushing the sheet away from her body.

She had a fucking perfect ass. Round globes I wanted to redden with my handprint while I thrust balls deep inside her puckered hole.

Jesus fuck.

I closed my eyes as my cock took an interest in the thoughts clouding my head. There probably wouldn't be any marking on her body. No handprints. No stripes from a flogger. No welts from my favorite cane.

She'd said she wanted to try, but how could pain possibly be her thing considering all she'd endured beneath Billy's manipulation and bruising fingertips? Could I live a vanilla lifestyle if my kink ended up turning her off?

Opening my eyes, I told myself I would be content with whatever she'd give.

Hand on her hip, I moved forward, gently cradling her backside with my body. Remnants of her sweet perfume lingered beneath the scent of the ocean clinging to her shoulder.

I ran my nose across her skin, breathing deep and filling my lungs. The soft strands of her hair caressed my face, and I nuzzled in, gently wrapping my arm around her.

She stiffened.

"It's me. Micah," I murmured. "You're safe."

She rubbed her hand along my forearm and sighed again, relaxing. "I fell asleep."

"Yes."

"Mmm." A slow stretch arched her ass against my cock, and I fought against the need to flex my hips.

"Are you sore?" I murmured over her ear.

"A little, but not too bad." Her low husky voice drew my balls up, and I slowly eased forward so the tip of my dick brushed over one of her rounded cheeks.

"You've got a great ass." I trailed my hand down her hip and over her top globe, squeezing and kneading rather than groping. I thought of my handprint on her ass again and rolled her to face me before I got carried away and I triggered her from being all over her backside like that fucker used to do.

She lifted her leg over my hip, spreading her open to help me forget about a good spanking. My fingers brushed over her pubic hair and slipped through the damp warmth beneath. Rimming her pussy hole brought a moan to her lips and coated my fingers with her cream.

"I love it when you touch me," she whispered, lifting a hand to grab hold of my head.

Given the green light, I pressed two fingers into her tight sheath, my cock jerking and smearing pre-cum on the back of her thigh. "You're so fucking wet. So tight." I pulled my fingers out and swept them up over her hard nub.

"Oh..." She arched into me.

I shifted lower on the bed, grabbed my cock, and angled between her spread thighs, rubbing myself against her soaked folds. "Do you want me?"

"God, yes." She yanked on my hair.

I flexed my hips and slid in deep inside her welcoming pussy with one slow thrust.

Jasmine groaned and shuddered.

"You like having my cock deep inside you."

"Yes."

I palmed her breast, pinching her hard nipple between two fingers. "How much?"

"Too much." She gasped as I thrust deep, hitting her cervix. "That hurts so damn good."

Oh fuck, those words on her tongue.

I pulled out to the head and thrust in again, drawing another deep groan from her, my hope buoyed. "I could fuck you all night long and not get enough."

"Yes," she whined as I pinched her nipple a little harder, writhing against me. "More."

"You do like a little pain, don't you?" I murmured against her neck, my fingers rolling her furled nub with enough pressure to make any human gasp.

Slickness coated my cock along with her moaned, "Yes, Sir."

"Jesus, Jasmine." I swallowed hard, sliding my hand down her back to pull her tight against me. I upped my pace, angling my hips to thrust deeper into her wet heat. Coating two fingers in her cream, I slid them up either side of her distended clit.

"Do you like it when I do this?" I asked, rubbing my fingers back and forth, her nub between them.

"O-oh, God!"

I tugged, gently pulling until her clit slipped from my grasp.

"Fuck!" She gasped, shuddering.

I tugged a little harder, and she shrieked, her pussy clamping on my cock. My fucking balls took over, and I gripped her hip, pounding into her soaked pussy with lewd, squelching noises, my teeth latching onto her shoulder.

"Fuck!" I growled against her skin as cum shot up through my cock.

"Micah!" Jasmine cried out again, sending another gush of wetness over my pulsing balls.

"Fucking hell, little lamb." I gulped, sucking wind. "Christ..."

I emptied myself inside of her, and my muscles went lax while I clung to her limp body.

Nothing in the fucking world would take her from me. Nothing. And I'd marked her shoulder with my teeth to let the world know who she belonged to.

Chapter 18

Jasmine

The scent of coffee pulled me from sleep. I blinked in the bright sunlight pouring through Micah's bedroom window and smiled.

I never smiled in the morning. Ever.

Stretching dissolved my jollity as the soreness between my thighs voiced a complaint. "Damn," I muttered. Micah's cock was a dangerous weapon. "Damn," I swore again while squeezing my thighs together a second time.

"You awake?"

I lifted my head off the pillow. "Unfortunately."

Micah stood in the open doorway, lounge pants slung low on his hips, showcasing that V of muscle that ought to be outlawed. His hair was a rumpled mess, and his sleepy eyes twinkled with enough heat I almost didn't care my pussy needed a break.

"You are so fucking hot," I moaned the words like a complaint.

He laughed and moved into the room. "I brought you some coffee."

I tore my gaze off the outline of his semi-hard cock and took note of the mugs in his hands. "You're a saint."

"Yeah, well..." He shrugged one shoulder.

Scooting up on the bed sent another not-so-pleasant twinge through my pussy, and I grimaced.

"You okay?" he asked, perching on the edge of the bed as I settled the sheet around my breasts.

Heat coated my cheeks. "A little sore."

"I shouldn't have taken you a second time," he said, handing me my coffee.

"I wanted you to."

He peered at me as I sipped and sighed contentment over the mug's rim.

I enjoyed another taste, humming my approval. "Best. Coffee. Ever."

With a chuckle, he slid back to prop against the headboard beside me. "How'd you sleep?"

"Like the dead. God." I shook my head. "I can't remember the last time I passed out like that."

"I know you like it bright in the room, so I left the blinds open." He rubbed his bare foot down the side of my sheet-covered calf. "Would it creep you out if I told you I laid here and watched you sleep for an hour before waking you up last night so I could have you again?"

Butterflies erupted into flight in my chest, and I glanced over at him. "You did?"

His gaze caressed my face, settling on my lips. "Yes. You're absolutely stunning—even when snoring."

"I don't snore!"

"You do."

I glared. "Do not."

He smirked. "Breathe heavy, then."

I huffed an exhale and turned away to drink my coffee.

"I got used to it pretty quick, and a good thing too."

Brow raised, I turned my head slightly. "Why's that?"

"'Cuz you're sleeping here every night from now on."

Heat flushed my body—arousal and annoyance at being told what to do clashing in my mind. "What?"

He smoothed a lock of crazy hair behind my ear. "You're moving in with me."

I barked a laugh, but his expression didn't waver. Tilting my head, I studied his serious-as-fuck gaze, still not sure of how to feel about his declaration. "Since when?"

"Since I said so."

"Is this when I'm supposed to act all submissive and say 'Yes, Sir?'" my mouth spewed before I thought the words through.

Fuck...the fire in his eyes. I swallowed and squeezed my thighs together, a luscious burn rooting deep inside my core.

"Your Sir should take you over his knee for speaking to him with that much sass."

Stifling silence swept in, ringing in my ears, and I didn't argue the title he'd claimed. Wetness seeped from my pussy, making it clear in my head what my body thought about him spanking me. But could my mind handle the controlled violence?

I tore my gaze from his and lifted my coffee to my lips with a trembling hand. While he'd been somewhat rough while fucking me during the night, I'd been too wrapped up in my need to think beyond his cock pounding into me and the release he could give me.

"Jasmine?" His voice had lost all trace of dominant alpha as he murmured my name. "Look at me."

His words didn't hold a demand for obedience, but I listened all the same.

"I won't ever lay a hand on you like that unless you want me to."

"But you do think about it, don't you?" I whispered, seeing the truth etched in his furrowed brow.

"Yes."

A heavy sigh lifted my chest. "I...I want to be that for you, Micah, but I don't know if I can. I said I'd be willing to try, and imagining it when I'm all hot and bothered...that comes easy. Without arousal included in the mix?" I shrugged, not wanting to speak the words that might make him set me aside in pursuit of someone better matching his lifestyle.

"I know." He toyed with a lock of my hair and let his hand fall limp on his lap, the coffee in his other hand seemingly forgotten. "I know," he repeated on a heavy sigh.

God, the defeat in his voice twisted a knife in my stomach. My throat tightened, and I turned away again.

"Hey." He gently grasped my chin and moved my head back around. "I'm okay with that. Honestly."

I stared at him as tears filled my eyes.

"Don't cry. Please." He rubbed his thumb down my cheek. "I'll gladly give up that lifestyle if it means I get to have you instead."

Gladly? I doubted it.

He dipped his head, peering into my eyes. "Alright?"

I made myself nod although I didn't *feel* okay.

A small smirk returned some of the light to his eyes. "How about a nice hot bath? That'll help with the soreness."

"Sounds good," I said, my voice low and scratchy.

"I'll draw the water for you." Micah slid off the bed and walked away, his tight ass flexing.

What we'd found together might be enough for a time. I

took another swallow of coffee. But he would grow bored with a vanilla sex life once the newness wore off.

What the fuck was I even thinking—we hadn't *discussed* a relationship. We hadn't agreed to an exclusive *anything* even though he'd claimed I was his in the heat of the moment and wanted me to call him Sir.

For all I knew, he could be fucking a different woman every other night. He owned an escort business for Christ's sake. Clients had probably acknowledged him in the same way.

He'd claimed I was his, but was that just part of the whole dominant side of him coming out while fucking? He'd also said I was moving in with him, but how long until he grew bothered by having someone all up in his space and told me to pack my shit and get out?

Damaged goods, I'd been labeled more than once. What man would want to deal with the shit baggage dragging along behind me?

Goddammit. I clenched my jaw and shut my eyes, fighting off tears. What the fuck was wrong with me? I needed to get a grip so his too-intuitive gaze didn't see the war tearing apart my insides. Drawing in a deep breath, I counted to ten. Ten to one on the exhale. Twice more, and the threat of tears dissipated. Another two, and assurance I could face him filled me.

I scooted off the bed, wincing. Good Lord Almighty, my pussy ached.

"Need me to carry you?" Micah asked as he returned to the bedroom.

A huff of laughter blew past my lips, and I fought against the rush of emotions again. "Nah." I grabbed my cover-up off of the floor and held it to my chest while sidling past him, intent on the bathroom.

"I'll bring you more coffee," he said as I stepped over the threshold onto the cool tile.

"Thanks, but I'll wait." I shut the door behind me and dropped the cover-up. Water poured from the spigot of his massive bathtub, steam rising in its wake.

I groaned while lowering myself into the hot water. So, so good…

A smile on my face, I lay back, closing my eyes. Micah's tub was easily twice the size of my parent's. My toes didn't even reach the other side.

Perhaps I ought to take advantage of Micah's offer for as long as he wanted to keep me around. He made coffee better than any barista, and his soft mattress cradled me ten times more tenderly than my old one at home. Never mind that every inch of his body was available for my enjoyment while I shared his bed.

The thought of other women in his life though turned off the arousal stirring in my blood.

We needed to have a little chat, one I didn't know how to start, let alone what all ought to be said. I just had to make the warring thoughts in my head shut the hell up so I could enjoy what I had—while I could.

It won't last.

That truth tightened my throat and spilled tears down my cheeks. Perhaps ending things before they developed into more would be the right choice. Regardless of what my mouth would spill once faced with him again, I knew I would eventually end up brokenhearted by the one man I longed to keep in my life.

Chapter 19

Micah

Jasmine lounged in the tub long enough I started to worry. If not for the quiet splash of water here and there, I'd have gone in to check on her. She'd seemed to need some space, though, so I had to give it.

I ran a hand over my jaw. Being unable to control a situation pissed me the hell off. She obviously didn't believe that I wanted her even if it meant no kink.

"Fucking hell." Using a little too much force, I stripped the sheets from my bed and remade it, fluffed the pillows, and tossed them back against the headboard.

"Jasmine?" I called through the bathroom door, unable to handle the distance between us for one second longer.

"Hmm?"

"I'll leave a T-shirt and shorts on the bed for you."

No fucking noise reached through the door.

"You hungry?" I asked.

"Sure."

"French toast, eggs, pancakes..."

"Whatever." Her bland, uninterested tone didn't help my mood.

I stalked to the kitchen and decided on scrambled eggs since I got to whip the hell out of them. A little bacon, a couple pieces of toast, and more coffee completed the meal.

"Breakfast is ready!" I hollered, having no clue what the fuck she was doing. "And," I muttered to myself, "I'm fucking starved, so I'm not waiting for you."

I wiped out the eggs and ended up cooking more, which sat and grew cold while I drank my third cup of coffee and watched sports talk radio on TV.

Jasmine finally made an appearance, but the food had gone cold. My cock stirred at the sight of her in my T-shirt hanging to the middle of her thighs and the pert breasts poking at the soft cotton.

"Want me to nuke it?" I asked, ambling back into the kitchen, empty mug in hand.

"Sure." She sat at the bar without looking at me, and I caught a flash of bare, upper thigh.

Of course my shorts would be too fucking big for her. The thought she might be panty-less sitting on the stool thickened me to full mast. Fucking cock didn't remember that I wasn't in the best of moods.

The microwave dinged, and I retrieved her breakfast and stood on the opposite side of the island to hide my tented lounge pants, sliding the plate over to her. "How was the bath?"

A small smile lifted her lips, lessening the knot in my gut the slightest bit. "Heavenly. Thank you."

"Hope you like scrambled eggs and bacon."

"Perfect." She pushed around the fluffy yellow bits before spearing a bite. Her lips parted, and I stared as she put the eggs in her mouth.

My fucking cock throbbed. I cleared my throat. "I

texted Dina to see if she would mind getting you some clothes."

Her brow lifted, and she finally glanced up at me. Eyes wary, unsure, she quickly returned her attention to her plate. "Why'd you do that?"

"Because I don't want Billy anywhere near you and don't like the idea of you going home."

"No piece of paper is going to stop him, and I can't hide the rest of my life, Micah."

"I'd feel better if he didn't know where you were at least."

She studied the piece of bacon in her hand, and tossed it onto her plate. "Look." A heavy sigh lifted her breasts. "I appreciate what you're trying to do, and last night was fantastic, but—"

"Don't, Jasmine."

Pain filled her eyes when she finally lifted her head. "This isn't going to work."

The fucking knife in my gut twisted. "Did I hurt you last night?"

"No."

"Was it too much? Too soon?" I ran a hand over my head. "You seemed so comfortable, so sure of yourself, that I felt we'd made progress."

"I did."

I peered at her a few second in silence, considering her words. "But *we* didn't," I clarified.

She tilted her head to the side, wetness coating her eyes. "What we, Micah? We have no commitment to each other. For all I know, you've been fucking women on the side, fulfilling that desire you have to dominate with pain since I'm unsure I can handle the full extent of your kinks."

Anger lit, and I fought to keep my jaw from clenching.

"There are no other women, Jasmine. Hasn't been since you stepped foot into my office. You're the only one. I want us." I motioned between her and me. "This. You and me. Together."

"What is *this*?" she asked without manipulation, her voice quiet and small.

"Surely you feel it," I said, trying to read the conflicting emotion in her pale-green eyes. "Tell me you don't notice that pull between us, that rightness when we're together. I told you last night you belonged to me, and you agreed."

Jasmine bit the inside of her lip.

"Look at me."

"I can't be the kind of partner you need," she whispered.

I straightened, having enough of her bullshit in not trusting me. "I don't need kink to be happy."

She peered up at me, offering a sad smile. "You say that now."

"I mean it."

"After all the women and your sexual experiences, you honestly think you'll be content with plain old vanilla sex? Me, a virgin as of a few hours ago?"

"There's nothing *plain* about the chemistry between us," I argued, having seen a shit ton of potential if she'd be willing to explore with me.

"I've never dated another man, so I wouldn't know if it's always like this—"

"It isn't."

"—but I agree there *is* something."

I wanted to drop to my knees and beg, but my cock still jutted out, and I wasn't about to let her see what a horny fuck I was. "Please stick around. I won't push. I won't ask."

"But you'll dream about it."

My lips pursed, and I nodded. "I won't lie that the idea of taking you over my lap and marking your ass with my hand doesn't turn me on."

She glanced away, shifting on the stool.

"You're afraid," I stated what I plainly saw on her face.

"Yes," she whispered, glancing up at me again.

"Do you trust me, Jasmine? Trust me to not hurt you?"

"Yes."

Relief poured over me, and the corners of my lips rose. "Then let's just take it one day at a time and see where things lead. I won't press. Ever. But if you decide someday that you want to try stuff outside vanilla, I'm willing." I dipped my head, my smile widening. "Whenever and wherever."

"You sure you're up for dealing with damaged goods on a daily basis?"

Chuckling, I rounded the island, and her gaze dropped to my tented lounge pants. "When it comes to you, Jasmine, I'll always be up." She giggled, and I cupped her cheek in my palm. "I'm falling for you. Hard. I can't even remember what life was like before I walked into the office and saw you three months ago."

Her eyes filled with tears again. "Same for me."

I leaned down and kissed her, slow and tender. She wound her fingers in my hair, tugging on the strands and sighing into my mouth.

The doorbell rang.

"Fuck," I growled, squeezing my cock and backing away. "*Worst* fucking timing."

Jasmine hopped off the stool and followed me to the front door.

I glanced out the window. "It's Dina."

"I'll get it." She motioned me toward the bedroom. "You go...take care of that."

"I'd rather if you did," I muttered.

Another giggle burst from her. "Later."

My brow rose along with a swell of hope in my chest. "Promise?"

She rolled her eyes and shoved me away from her. "Promise. Now, get out of here. I don't want my sister ogling the goods."

Chuckling, I turned, giving her some privacy to chat with her sister and me time to calm my dick the fuck down.

Chapter 20

Jasmine

"Well." Dina's brows rose as she took in my messy hair and Micah's T-shirt covering me to mid-thigh. "You look like you were ridden hard and put to bed wet."

Heat flooded my face, and I stepped back.

"I know you don't have anything to compare him to, but was he any good?" she murmured, passing me and scanning the living room. "Can't say I haven't wondered."

"Ten times better than I imagined it would be," I admitted.

She dropped the two trash bags she'd carried in and turned to face me, her scrutiny making my feet shift. "How are you?"

I struggled for words to explain the happiness and lingering wariness but settled on a single word. "Great."

"Are you?"

"Yes, Dina." I smiled. "Honestly."

She nodded and looked around again. "Where is he?"

"Getting dressed."

Her brows shot up again as she glanced down once

more at his shirt and my bare breasts jutting out at her. "I hope I didn't interrupt."

I bit the inside of my lip to keep from giggling.

"Never mind." She waved her hand. "Forget I said anything."

"Want some coffee?" I asked, moving around her toward the kitchen.

"We need to meet with the florist in an hour to finalize everything."

"Shit," I muttered, having lost track of the days—hours. Hell, months if I was honest with myself. Micah had consumed me—

"You forgot." Dina made a statement rather than questioning my curse.

"Yes." I glanced over my shoulder to find her nodding and pulled up short of the coffeepot.

"Shouldn't be surprised with the events of the last twenty-four hours," she grumbled and heaved a sigh. "Liz's babysitter backed out, but Mom and I can handle the meeting alone. You can stay here and do...whatever I interrupted."

"No, I want to go. It'll only take me a few minutes to throw some clothes on." I hurried past her, grabbed the trash bags, and hefted them toward the bedroom. "Give me five, okay?"

Dina smiled, and it seemed some of the wedding stress melted off her shoulders. "Thank you."

Micah was in the bathroom, so I upended one bag onto the bed and grabbed the first pair of jean shorts and tank top I saw. Panties and bras—all of the pretty ones, I noted—lay in the bottom of the second bag and spilled out over the comforter.

Grinning at my sister's thoughtfulness, I tugged Micah's

shirt off and pulled on a pair of black, lacy panties and a matching bra.

"Please tell me you're not heading out and leaving me all alone with this memory imprinted in my brain."

Micah stood in the bathroom doorway, cock still tenting his pants, his stare on the little piece of black lace covering my pussy.

"I forgot we're scheduled to go to the florist today."

"Damn." He slipped his hand inside his pants and stroked his length.

Heat pooled between my thighs, and I tore my gaze off him to tug up the jean shorts.

"Mmm," he moaned, sending a rush of fire through my blood.

"Stop it," I whispered, glancing at the closed bedroom door.

"Don't want to."

I threw a mock glare his way and pulled on the tank top. "Do what you have to, then," I said, hands on hips, "but you better be ready again for later. I've got a promise to keep."

The need in his gaze slammed into me, catching my breath.

"Always," he stated, stalking across the room toward me.

Tension suddenly slammed into me at how he moved— but I kept my face on his, reminding me of who approached.

I held my ground as he hesitated, reading me like an open book.

"Jasmine?"

"Green," I whispered.

He cradled my face in his hands and claimed my mouth, making my knees go weak in a matter of seconds. "Be careful," he murmured against my lips as I sagged against him. "Don't be alone at any time for any reason. Please."

"I won't." I pulled back and smiled up at him, knowing my five minutes had ticked past and then some.

"You'd better," he said, stepping away, hand once more going to his cock.

"Or?" I asked with a saucy smirk.

His brow arched as a glint lit his eyes. "Little minx. You're asking for trouble."

The image he'd created in my mind earlier flitted to life, and I shivered at the thought of being over his knee, his hands smoothing over my bare skin. He would make it hurt like his teeth on my nipples, his firm tugs on my clit that had sent me soaring. Pain with Micah so far had equaled intense pleasure. I could trust him to continue on in the same vein.

Perhaps I'd be ready to test out a little kink sooner than I expected.

JE

"God, I just want this wedding to be done. Over with."

I giggled at Dina as she slumped into a booth at the steak house we'd decided on for a late lunch. "You and Aaron should have just gotten hitched in Mom and Dad's backyard."

"I wish to hell we had." She flagged down the closest waiter as Mom slid in beside her, leaving me alone as I preferred. "Are you our waiter?" she asked as the young man stopped beside our table.

"No, but I can get her."

"I need a glass of chardonnay, like yesterday," Dina said, smiling brightly up at him. "Think you can hook me up or relay the message for me?"

I rolled my eyes and grabbed the menu the host had laid on the table before shuffling off. The breakfast Micah had cooked for me hadn't all made its way to my stomach, and hunger pains twisted and gurgled.

Flat iron steak, salad with blue cheese...I flipped a page back to the inside cover...a platter of pepper shrimp. I dropped the menu, scanning for a waiter. "I'm so damn hungry I could eat a raw tomato."

Mom laughed. "The day you eat a raw tomato is the day I find myself pregnant again."

Dina snorted at me. "'Cuz you worked up an appetite between last night and this morning."

Heat flamed my face, and I picked up the menu to hide behind as Mom lifted her attention off the specials list she held, glancing between us. We had always had an open relationship when it came to personal things. There wasn't much my mom didn't know about my life.

"Jasmine?" she said, and I sighed, lowering the menu as she did the same with the paper she held. "Did you, um..."

"Yes, Mom."

She clasped a hand over her mouth, eyes wide. "My God! You actually...you know." She fluttered her free hand while mumbling around her palm.

"Twice."

Her eyes went even wider. "And?"

I expected she wasn't asking how the sex was but asking about my response. Although I fidgeted in the booth, I smiled. "Not a single tingle of anxiety."

"Plenty of other tingles though, I'm sure," Dina said, snickering.

I shot her a glare, but the waitress arrived, glass of wine in hand for my thirsty sister.

"I'll take one of those," I said.

"Well." Mom straightened, her voice breathless. "I believe I will too. It would seem we have things to celebrate!"

For the first time, I sat and whispered about sex with firsthand knowledge. Liz would be upset about missing out our luncheon and the topic of discussion.

My phone dinged, and I dug it from my purse.

Micah: **Miss you.**

I turned my phone so Mom could see his message.

She slumped against the booth, a hand on her heart and eyes filling with tears.

"Never thought I'd see the day," Dina said, swallowing down the last of her third glass of wine. "Micah Fox, smitten with a woman." She shook her head but smiled. "If he hurts you, I swear to God..."

I nodded, love and appreciation for my big sister swelling in my chest. My fingers flew over the screen as I told him the same and that I would head back to my parents to grab my car before heading home to him.

Home.

Biting the inside of my lip, I put my phone back in my purse. "Do you think it's too much, too soon?" I asked, settling my gaze on Mom.

"You're definitely caught up in the newness of life right now, but if you both agree on what you're feeling and what you want, then no."

I nodded, twirling the wine glass stem in my fingers. "I'm falling in love with him."

Neither Dina nor Mom said anything, and I glanced between them as my phone dinged again.

Dina shrugged. "When you know, you know."

"How long were you with Aaron before you concluded he was the one?" I grabbed my cell again.

"First date."

My brows shot up as I scanned Micah's request to be careful. "Really?"

"Me too," Mom said.

"I never knew that." I smiled, tossed my phone back in my purse, and propped my elbow on the table so I could rest my chin in my hand.

"Sixth grade." Mom's crooked smile lit her face. "I'd just learned where babies came from, and Lordy, did I want to have your daddy's."

The three of us giggled, and I realized neither Mom nor Dina would be able to drive home with all of the wine they'd drunk. A half hour later, we climbed into Dina's car —me driving—and headed to my parents. While there, I packed up a few personal things I didn't want to be without.

Dad was concerned over my moving in with Micah so quickly even if it was only until the Billy issue resolved itself, but said the decision was mine to make. He trusted me and my instincts. He also trusted Dina's word that Micah was a decent man and wouldn't hurt or take advantage of me.

I'd been smiling most of the morning, and my damn face ached. Warmth spread through my body as I pulled into Micah's long driveway. Had he waited for me to put my lips on his cock, or had he masturbated while fantasizing about me? The thought of both soaked my panties.

I couldn't wait to find out.

Chapter 21

Micah

I paced, glancing out the window every couple of minutes. I'd almost texted Jasmine to find out where she was, but didn't want her trying to text and drive at the same time. I peered down the driveway again, and a rush of relief loosened the tension in my body at seeing her old Camry turn into the driveway.

While I didn't want to appear the worrywart, I ended up hurrying out the front door anyway. She climbed from the car, her face glowing, sunlight glinting off the golden streaks in her blonde hair.

I held out my arms, and she threw herself against me, lips and tongue greedy on mine.

My cock sprang to attention, and I lifted her up into my arms, palming her ass. "You're my addiction," I groaned against her mouth while pressing my cock against her soft core.

"And you're mine," she whispered, pulling back, her pale eyes filled with need. "I'm glad to feel you're more than ready for me."

"I waited."

She arched a brow and speared her fingers through my hair. "You did?"

"Yeah." I brushed my lips across hers. "But now I'm in pain because of it."

Her giggle bounced her breasts against me, and I squeezed her ass with a groan. "Blame it on Dina and my mom. We ended up talking for three hours over lunch."

"Did you have a good time?" I asked and nibbled along her jaw, grinding my hips against her.

"Mmm."

I turned and carried her inside, my brain cursing that she wore jean shorts rather than an easy-access skirt. A fuck up against a wall sounded downright sweet at the moment. Once inside the house, I slid her down along my body to her feet.

"I brought some stuff from my parents," she murmured, her hands on my chest.

"We'll get it later," I said, snapping open the button on her jean shorts.

"Hmm." Her brows arched as I pushed the shorts and her panties from her hips. "So what do you have in mind that's so important my personal belongings melt from this heat in my car?" she asked, stepping out of them.

I shoved my shorts down, freeing my throbbing cock, and kicked them off. "This." I picked her back up, and she wrapped her legs around me. The need to thrust deep into her tight pussy rolled over me, setting my blood on fire, but she still had to be sore from the night before.

Easy, I reminded myself, leaning her back against the front door and flexing my hips to rub my cock through her soaked folds. "I'm going to get off like this—don't want to hurt you."

"Mmm," she moaned, tipping her head against the door,

eyes closing. "Don't hold back, Micah. Please put your dick inside me again if me sucking your cock needs to wait."

"Fuck." I slid into her tightness and stilled as she gasped, my body trembling with the desire to take her hard and fast.

Jasmine lifted her head, and I caught a glimpse of passion-hazed green eyes before she crushed her mouth to mine.

Green fucking light to plunder.

I backed out and slammed in, drawing a groan from her chest. My fingers dug into her ass cheeks, the hot slickness of her tight pussy driving me fucking insane. I couldn't get close enough. Deep enough.

"Oh, fuck, Jasmine." I groaned into her neck, my hips rocking into her as my cock tried to split her in half. "So. Fucking. Good."

She shuddered in my arms, pulled on my hair, and squeezed her inner walls around me as I grazed my teeth over her jawline, her soft neck. I wanted to mark her up. Bite indentations. Suck purple bruises along her skin that would catch her breath every time she touched them.

"I'm going to come," she gasped, arching her back and pusher her breasts closer to me.

Hard nipples poked out, and I dipped my head, clamping my teeth onto one.

A shriek ripped from Jasmine's lips, and she came hard, her cum leaking around my thrusting length.

"Goddamn..." I stabbed into her a few more times, trying like hell to draw out her climax, but my balls gave up the fight, and I hollered. My knees almost buckled as I shot my cum deep inside her.

"Mmm." She heaved for breath, moistening her top lip with the tip of her tongue. "My first fuck against a door.

Damn." Her body went lax in my arms, and I half-stumbled into the kitchen, sitting her ass on the counter by the sink and pulling out of her warmth.

I spread her thighs and glanced down.

"Mine," I said, trailing a finger up through my cum and rubbing it over every inch of her reddened pussy and clit.

"Yes," she whispered, her hands twining in the mess she'd made of my hair as I leaned forward to brush my lips over hers.

A shuddering sigh wracked through her body. "We definitely have to do that again."

"I want you bent over the couch next."

"Oh, God, yes." Her nails dug into my scalp.

I chuckled and kissed her again. "Give me a couple minutes to recoup first, though."

She huffed a fake sigh. "Fine."

"Let's clean up, grab your stuff from the car, and see if you can handle another round."

Ten minutes later, I grabbed two of the three boxes out of the trunk of her car, cursing the fucking heat. I passed Jasmine on the walkway. "Five more minutes, and your ass is mine," I said over my shoulder as she went to the car to get the last box.

"Promise?" she called back, her voice saucy and taunting.

I groaned with the desire to redden her backside but kept moving to the bedroom where I sat the boxes on the bed. Hand dropping to stroke my cock through my shorts, I turned around, eyeing the bed. *Our* bed. Maybe I would spread her out like a feast and devour every inch of her luscious body instead of a quickie over the back of the—

"Micah!" Jasmine screamed, terror in her voice.

I took off, tearing across the living room, heart in my throat, and skidded to a stop in the doorway.

Jasmine's back was pressed against the door of her Camry, a box of possessions scattered around her feet, and a fat fuck who had to be the asshole Billy waved a knife a foot away from her face.

Fucking. Red.

"Jasmine!" Fists clenched, I took in Billy's unsteady stance, his straggly hair, his pasty complexion—all within a single heartbeat as my holler turned his focus my way.

Jasmine ducked and sprinted toward the rear of the car, and I leaped down the stairs in one bound, feet pounding the walkway as the fat fuck chased after her.

She rounded the trunk of the Camry, terror in her eyes as she stumbled toward me along the passenger side, Billy on her heels.

I reached her before he did and yanked her behind me.

Billy drew up quick for the weight he carried, the knife raising once more in his fist mere feet from me. "Little lying *cunt*." He spat on my driveway, and I backed up, trying not to stumble over Jasmine as she clung to the back of my shirt, whimpering. "I'm going to cut out your fucking tongue and shove it up your ass."

"You touch her," I said, my voice calm as fuck, "and you're a dead man."

His pinned eyes scanned down my front as he shifted his weight. "Gonna kill me with your bare hands, pretty boy?"

"Yes," I stated the truth, plain and simple. I didn't care if he buried the damn knife hilt-deep in me while I did as I'd vowed. I would end his fucking life before he put his hands on Jasmine again.

"Then come on." Billy grinned and waved his knife. "Come and get me if you think you can take me."

"D-Don't," Jasmine whispered, tugging on my shirt.

"Get in the house," I told her without taking my eyes off the asshole. "Call 911."

She hesitated.

"Now isn't the time to disobey me, Jasmine," I growled.

Still, she hesitated, and I swore to myself if Billy didn't end up sticking that knife in a vital organ, I'd redden her ass whether she wanted me to or not.

Billy's grin widened, and he beckoned toward me with his free hand. "Come on, pansy-ass. All them muscles are just show. You ain't got shit on me." He spat again. "I'm a badass motherfucker. Done time." His eyes went psycho, and like an absolute moron, he spread his arms wide, leaving himself vulnerable. "I'm a fucking—"

I leaped forward, my right hook slamming into his jaw before he could bring the knife back in front of him. His head snapped to the side, and he went down in a heap, the blade clattering on the driveway.

Anticlimactic as fuck but satisfying all the same.

Jasmine gasped behind me, but I stared down at Billy, wanting him to get up so I could punch him in the fucking head again.

He didn't stir except for the slight rise and fall of his chest.

"Call 911, Jasmine," I repeated, my fists still clenched, my ears ringing as I towered over the scum of the earth who thought to fuck with my woman.

I glanced over my shoulder. Jasmine hadn't moved. She stood trembling, hands over her ears, widened eyes staring at the asshole at my feet.

"Jasmine," I said, forcing my voice to calm. "He's out

cold and not coming to any time soon. I won't let him touch you."

She tore her focus off him and met my gaze, dropping her arms to wrap around her waist to hug herself tight.

I tried for a reassuring smile although I lusted to fucking rip the fucker to shreds. "You're all right. Be strong like you have been the past couple of months. You can do this. I have faith in you."

She nodded, took a stumbling step backward, and hurried into the house.

I turned my attention back on Billy who hadn't moved. "Fucking piece of shit," I hissed. "You're lucky I hit you in the jaw and didn't crush your nose clear into your brain like I wanted to."

My spiked adrenaline hadn't gotten completely used up, and I fought against the need to shake. I opened and flexed the hand I'd crushed his jaw with. It fucking hurt.

But was better than a stab wound any day.

Chapter 22

Jasmine

I had nightmares for three days in a row.

Micah's security cameras caught Billy in the act of sneaking up on me as I'd used my hip to shut my car's back door. He'd humped against my backside like he'd done as a kid before I'd even realized someone stood behind me.

My restraining order still stood, and he'd directly violated it. Add in the blade he'd had in hand while threatening my life along with Micah's, and Billy wouldn't be free again for a long time.

But my mind instinctively tossed my emotions into a slammer of sorts along with him.

Dry-eyed, I curled in on myself, unable to work or even function. My parents suggested I move back home, but I felt safer in Micah's house even though every time he had reached for me in the hours following the attack, I'd flinched. He'd stopped trying after the third attempt, giving me space.

I hadn't broken down but had gone from shock to stoic

silence. Bottled up tight. I slept in the guest room. Alone. Lights on.

The fourth night I woke gasping for breath, Micah stood in the doorway, knuckles white from how he grasped the doorjamb.

My heart pounded, but I swallowed against rising emotions while shaking my head. "I-I'm fine."

"You're *not* fine," he snapped, eyes glinting. "You need to cry. Scream while you're awake. Beat on me—something! At least call your therapist like Dina has been begging you to do!"

I balked against his suggestions, clinging to the sense of security I felt by shoving all the shit down deep. "C-Can't."

A muscle ticked in Micah's jaw. He stared at me with longing and concern, unlike my parents' pitying gazes.

The flash of Billy pressing up against me in my mind made me open my eyes wider as I grew desperate to escape the images. "I don't *want* to remember it anymore." My eyes watered without permission as I relived the feel of Billy's hardness digging into my backside and his guttural groan I'd had echoing in my head since childhood. "I can't stop thinking about it—even when I'm asleep! How can I make it go away?" I bit hard on my tongue to keep sobs restrained.

Regardless, a tear slid down my face onto the T-shirt I'd worn for two days straight, but I fought to stuff it down. Take back the power.

I am strong. I am able to overcome...

Micah drew near, hands flexing at his sides as though desperate to reach out to me. "I would touch you if I could. Give you a million other things to focus on. Pleasure. Pain if that's what you want. Bliss."

He hurt. I could see it in his eyes, in the stoop of his shoulders.

I'd beaten Billy's shit once before because of the man before me. I'd been determined to live a new life where affection was welcome, but I'd allowed Billy to once more dictate my thoughts and actions.

Memories of Micah's arms, his gentle touch wavered through the shit in my head.

My stomach churned as I realized what I'd been missing out on the previous three days—what I hadn't allowed myself to seek comfort in. He stood before me. Willing— always so open and ready to give me whatever I needed.

I *needed* to forget. To live. To submerge myself in all things Micah to drown out the negative.

Pulse picking up speed, I slid off the bed, my bare feet on the plush rug. The fibers felt soft, a gentle caress on my soles and toes. The pleasant sense grounded me, gave me thorough clarity of what I wanted.

Micah eyed me as I shuffled toward him, his gaze wary.

I stopped in front of him, electrical charges seeming to zap between the short distance separating us. "I'm sorry for flinching away from you."

"It's alright," he murmured.

"It's *not*," I insisted, my focus sliding down his neck to his bare chest. Rippled muscles made my mouth water.

As though knowing where my mind went, Micah clasped his hands behind his back, promising me he wouldn't touch—telling me I could.

I pressed my palm to his heart, the familiar heat of him seeping up through my arm. My breath left in a rush as my eyelashes fluttered downward.

"Okay?"

I nodded, swallowing against the thickness in my throat that bore no resemblance to panic.

We stood in silence a few long moments, both of our

exhales loud in the stillness. Eventually, I calmed enough to raise my head. Crystalline blue...desire...apprehension met my gaze.

Micah would never hurt me.

Warmth slid through my body, and I shuddered at the sensation of arousal.

"Jasmine," he whispered as a tremor rippled through him.

I lifted my other hand and palmed his firm pecs. A sense of security, rightness, settled over me. "I need to kiss you."

Micah backed away from me, but kept his focus on my face as he sat on the chair a few feet away. He set his hands on his thighs, fingers splayed. "Come here, little lamb."

Goose bumps rose over my arms at his tone, and I moved on autopilot to stand between his spread thighs. Lounge pants covered his lower body but didn't hide how I affected him.

Nibbling on my lower lip, I stopped just shy of touching him.

He tiled his head back slightly, waiting for me to decide what to do.

I found myself obeying my body's yearning without thought, leaning in to brush my dry lips over his.

Micah didn't move, simply sat still and allowed me to initiate, to touch, without interference. But, I could feel the tension in him radiating like the summer sun's rays heating me through.

"Micah," I whispered, "give me your tongue.

With a soft groan, he licked gently over my lower lip.

I whimpered and opened, my hands finding his scruffy cheeks. The prickle of his stubble kept me focused on who kissed me. The only man to own my mouth, the only lover to make my body sing.

Memories of his soothing hands that brought blinding pleasure swelled inside my mind with every swipe of his tongue against mine, obliterating all other thoughts. His low moan made shivers slide over my skin. His panted exhales filled my lungs, reminding me of everything I'd found in his arms.

"Touch me," I murmured, pulling back just enough to see his passion-hazed eyes.

Tentative fingers feathered over my hips.

"I'm green," I whispered.

Micah's touch solidified, palms pressing against my skin.

Caught up in him, the truth of who he was to me—that I could be with him without emotional pain—dictated my moves.

I slid onto his lap, my core aching. "You make me forget."

He studied me a moment, his body completely still except for the rise and fall of his chest. "I'm not going to be your escape. You can't hide from what happened, Jasmine."

Indignation flared, and I frowned, stiffening. Didn't he notice steps I'd just taken? The choice I had remembered in my head that made a physical connection between us possible?

A slow smirk curved his lips, pissing me off even more.

"I break through after three days of living in bullshit emotions, and you're going to deny me?" Huffing, I started to pull away, but Micah's hold on my hips tightened. "Let me go," I hissed, ready to smack him across his gorgeous smiling face.

"Do you trust me?"

I blinked, my frown deepening. "You know I do."

"Who's touching you right now?' His hands slid around my backside, his hold firm yet gentle.

"You are," I answered, my pissiness lessening slightly at his soothing tone.

"Say my name."

What was he up to?

"Micah," I answered with more than a hint of sass.

"*Who* am I?"

"My boss. Friend. Lover."

He lifted an eyebrow as though waiting for one title I may have forgotten.

I heaved a heavy exhale, the fight leaving me as I realized what he hoped to hear. "Sir," I whispered my submission.

His heating gaze slid over my face, settling on my lips. "What's your safeword, little lamb?"

My pulse heightened, and I licked my lower lip at the determination in his steady gaze. "Red," I whispered.

"And who is in control?" he asked, his focus flitting up to my eyes once more.

Whatever negative emotions had stirred in the previous few minutes settled into placid waters at his gentle reminder.

"I am," I stated quietly, mentally sliding into the calm lake waiting to offer me relief.

That damn smirk appeared again but whipped from my vision a heartbeat later as I found myself draped over his lap, head hanging, toes barely touching the floor.

Flight instincts tightened my muscles, but his warm palm slid over my ass cheeks, keeping me in place.

"Relax," he crooned...and I did at his low tone, all the air leaving my lungs. "It's time to let go, Jasmine."

"Micah..."

"Do you trust me?" he asked again, sliding his hand up beneath my shirt to palm one cheek through my cotton panties.

I knew what he planned. Expected his loving pain to offer me emotional release I needed but had refused to allow myself out of fear. I'd given Billy power over me, and Micah would show me how to take it back.

"Yes, Sir." I closed my eyes.

The first swat registered in my ears before the slight sting rose on my skin. I gasped, blinking my eyes open. Micah's hand felt nothing like the wooden spoon and belt I'd gotten as a kid. And the soft caress immediately afterward on tingling flesh?

Oh wow.

"Color?"

I licked my lower lip. "Green."

Another smack hit my other cheek, sending a shiver of arousal through my core.

"More," I whispered.

Another blow...a fourth. Fifth.

Rather than sinking into bliss like I'd read about though, I began to tense against the swelling inside my chest, the cracking of the box I thought I'd emptied everything inside.

"Jasmine."

"Don't stop." I shuddered, my throat tightening along with the rest of my muscles. "Please."

Two more blows, and I whimpered, shifting against his legs.

My eyes burned. I knew I could stop it all with one word, but I'd had enough. It was time. "I-I'm good," I promised, my body trembling as the fissure inside me widened.

Micah's palm soothed over my hot backside, dipping down between my thighs.

He groaned as his fingertips danced over my damp slit.

"P-Please, Sir," I begged, eyes clenched tight.

One hand on my lower back kept me focused on what I needed to do. Grounded in the moment with *who* I'd entrusted myself to. Micah's other palm landed on the top of my thigh, and I jolted forward, a sob ripping from me. Another heavy hand enticed a second cry to pour from my lips. A third caused all the shit I'd attempted to hide from to erupt.

"M-Micah—" My voice broke along with my restraint. I fell the fuck apart.

"That's it, sweet girl." Micah pulled me into his arms, and I clung to his broad shoulders, knowing he would protect me while I loosened all the demons from inside their prison.

Chapter 23

Micah

Jasmine clung to me like I was a buoy in the storm sea she fought to keep from drowning in.

I kept my hold light, face in her hair, breathing in the natural sweet scent of her. My girl broke apart after almost four days of cold silence that had drained her face of color and body of energy.

I'd felt helpless every hour, watching her suffer from afar. The first day, I'd attempted to hug her before the cops had even arrived, but she'd stepped back, arms wrapped around herself. A soft touch to her lower back an hour later had made her gasp and scuttle away as though I'd burned her skin.

The third time, I'd intentionally grazed her elbow, and she'd gone into a full-blown panic attack that had taken us counting out breaths for ten minutes before she'd calmed.

I hadn't touched her since, thinking sure that fuck head had broken Jasmine for good.

But I finally figured out it was fear ruling her reactions rather than her mind. I'd seen her strength. Her determination. She'd simply needed to be reminded of the power she held—in sceneing and otherwise.

Her tears soaked my skin, and rather than pity or have my heart break for her sorrow, I took pleasure in it. Add in the fact my spanking her gorgeous ass had aroused her body regardless of her emotional state, and hope blossomed in my head that we might one day get to where I'd like to be.

I doubted Jasmine would ever want the cane, but I could live without the hardcore shit. Maybe a flogger... crop...I could easily envision both moving over her skin and would find contentment in giving her release every fucking time she allowed it.

Maybe I would take her to Chantelle's one night, allow her to see the lifestyle in living color. Watch her reactions to different scenes. Find what else might turn my little innocent lamb on.

But in the meantime, I would hold her. Comfort her. Be a rock she could huddle upon when things got too deep to wade through on her own.

"So fucking proud of you, Jasmine." I kissed her head, soothing my hands on her arm and thigh until she eventually quieted.

A month earlier, I would have allowed her space, to dictate our next moves, but my woman needed to be reminded of my intentions. My growing love for her. My determination to stick with her through whatever shit roused to threaten what we'd found together.

She knew her safeword, and I trusted her to use it if I misjudged what else she needed.

Standing, I kept her tight against my chest.

With a sigh, she snuggled in closer, nose on my neck, her exhales hot on my skin.

My dick swelled with every sure step taking me down

the hallway toward our bedroom. Using my elbow, I flipped on the lights, illuminating the corners of the room.

I set Jasmine on her feet, her wet eyes green as spring grass and vulnerable as fuck.

Lust kicked through my groin, and I clenched my jaw rather than ravaging her mouth. Without a word, I lifted her T-shirt—and she let me toss it aside without a sound. I glanced down over her body, the curves of her breasts, her taut belly, and the plain white panties that never ceased to drive me insane.

The fucker had warped her mind when it came to having me behind her, but it was time for my woman to take back all control. No more fucking hinderances.

"Take off those panties and turn around, little lamb."

She shuddered and stared at me.

I kept silent, knowing she would find the courage to obey.

Her throat worked as she swallowed. "I...I'll need to hear your voice if I can't see you, Micah."

"I won't let you forget who's loving on you," I promised.

A shuddered sigh ripped through Jasmine, and she nodded, slowly stripping down and turning.

"On your knees on the bed. Face the headboard."

She moved with hesitant footsteps but climbed onto the mattress like a good girl. Head bowed, she rested her hands on her thighs, the curve of her lower back and her reddened ass making my dick buck hard in my lounge pants.

I shoved them to my ankles and left them lying on the floor.

"No pain this time," I spoke quietly while climbing onto the bed beside her. "Nothing but pleasure for my little lamb." I swept her hair over her shoulder, my fingertips grazing her neck. "You're so goddamned beautiful.

Every inch of your skin...shoulders...spine...the curve right here."

While speaking, I trailed my soft touch over her body, mapping out every delicious inch.

Goose bumps slid down her arms, and she whimpered as I caressed over the redness on her ass cheeks.

"You were so brave for me. So strong—but I know you have more in you. We're going to break his hold once and for all, Jasmine."

I hated to even bring up the fucker in that moment, but I didn't want her sinking into pleasure without recognizing *she* had chosen to push toward healing, that I wasn't just a mere bandage.

"Hands on the headboard," I said, shifting to settle directly behind her, my palm resting on her hip.

She obeyed, head still lowered.

"Up on your knees."

A quiet whimper left her, but I praised her slow effort to please me.

"So fucking gorgeous," I murmured, going on to tell her in detail about my handprints on her tanned skin, how arousing the marks she'd allowed me to give her were.

Wetness glistened along her slit, and I hummed my approval while gliding a single fingertip through the slickness. "You're wet for me."

"Always," she whispered. Her back arched slightly as I rimmed her pink hole, a green light I wasn't about to slow down for.

I pushed into her tight sheath, immediately going for her G spot. "So wet and warm," I groaned the words, caressing my other hand over her hip and thigh. "Gonna bury my dick inside you. Stay for fucking forever, little lamb."

Jasmine shuddered, moaning as I stroked over the roughened patch deep in her core.

"Spread your thighs for me, baby."

She did as told, offering me an even better view of her entire backside.

"Goddamn." My mouth watered to taste every inch of her from clit to puckered hole. I didn't care if she hadn't changed or showered in two days. That moment wasn't about fulfilling my lusts but reminding her of the pleasure she could take. Own.

Still murmuring about how much she pleased me, how her strength impressed me, I slid my finger from her body, smearing her wetness over my leaking cock. I moved in closer, rubbing the swollen head of my dick through her lower lips and up her crack, smearing her arousal all the fuck over.

One day...I would claim that hole too.

I slid down to her pussy and flexed my ass, slowly sinking into her tight heat. "Fuck, Jasmine." I hissed through clenched teeth while seating myself fully inside her body. A shudder ripped through me, and I whispered nonstop while sliding my hands up her sides to grasp her breasts.

"So soft. Delicious." I tweaked her nipples without thrusting, simply keeping her focused on the now.

"Micah." No hesitancy laced her tone, only need.

"I have you, Jasmine. Gonna make you fly."

She whimpered.

"Just stay with me, okay? Don't forget whose hands are on you—that it's my dick your body is weeping for."

I slid out until my glans appeared but pressed back in fully. "Jesus. You feel so fucking good." I repeated the motion, cursing again once I buried deep. "Whose cock is throbbing against your womb, baby?"

"You—shit. Micah. You're so deep inside me."

I wouldn't ever delve into her as thoroughly as I would prefer, but I would take what I could.

"Who am I?"

"Sir," she didn't hesitate to answer.

A rumbled approval rose from my chest, and I pulled Jasmine up against me. One hand grasped in her hair, I tipped her head to the side to give me access to her neck while I pushed into her with shallow thrusts.

"Fucking love it when you call me that," I groaned, sliding my other hand between her splayed thighs as she grasped hold of my hips. "Love how your body responds to me." Wetness coated my wandering fingers, and I rubbed over her clit. "Love those little whimpers on your lips too."

Her arousal slid over my balls, making for one hell of a messy, slow fuck. And I kept up with the praise, teasing her clit. Letting up when she started to pant. Sweat rose between my chest and her back, and I ground against her ass intentionally, keeping her tight against me while spilling all sorts of erotic words in her ear.

Jasmine stayed with me through every drawn out moment, every second that ticked by. Her fingernails dug into my skin, and her body trembled against me.

"Want you to come all over my cock, beautiful." I tugged on her clit, just shy of too hard.

She moaned, writhing against my groin. "Need it."

"Gonna give it to you—promise. Trust me?"

"Yes—fuck, yes I do."

I spun us and pushed forward, sprawling her out long-ways across the mattress. Blanketing her entire backside, I pressed her thighs wide with my legs.

"Love everything about you, Jasmine." I thrust hard, thrumming my fingertips over her clit. I bit on the soft flesh of her neck, lapping and sucking while stabbing into her pussy. "So strong in your submission. Fucking perfect for me."

The sounds of slapping flesh rose to combat the noises leaving her mouth, the deep moans and curses that let me know she chose to stay with me, that she kept focused on who brought her pleasure.

"Ready to come for me?" I asked, angling my hips to take her even deeper.

"Fuck yes."

"Then come." I pinched her clit and bit down on her shoulder.

Wetness gushed over my dick and balls, and I cursed as my taint spasmed. "Fuck—gonna fill you up, baby. Shit." I gasped and shuddered as cum erupted up through my shaft. A low groan and I spurted again. And again. "Jesus—fuck." I gulped and lifted to watch every stuttered thrust as I emptied inside her.

"Fucking hell, Jasmine." Sucking oxygen, I stayed buried inside her and rolled us onto our sides. My face in her hair, I nuzzled, my palm over her thumping heart. "Okay?"

"More than," she murmured, twining her fingers through mine. A shudder relaxed her further into my hold.

"Never letting you go," I warned her.

She didn't argue.

Chapter 24

Jasmine

Three weeks later...

Days passed, and with every dawn, the truth of reality and my future solidified in my mind. Billy was officially charged and sent back to prison for ten years with no hope for parole. I went back to work. Micah and I settled into a routine, one that was comfortable and oftentimes arousing as fuck. Occasionally, I had setbacks, especially if something rose to remind me of Billy and Micah's touch caught me off guard.

But we made progress. I moved forward on my own as well as alongside him.

I annoyed him at times and vice versa whenever two people invaded each other's space on a full-time basis, but we ended up giggling about toothpaste splatter on the mirror and dirty socks in front of the hamper instead of inside it.

The true test rose three weeks after the attack when Micah's family came over for dinner. My nerves sat on high alert, making me jumpy and skittish. No matter how much he assured me they would adore everything about me, I worried how my body would react in greeting them.

I should have known better.

Micah's mom was sweet, smiling and blowing me a kiss from afar rather than hugging me. His dad seemed depressed, but Micah had warned me about his health issues and how he dealt with them regardless of his liver shutting down. The older, silver fox image of Micah—my swooning insides—arrived at our house already half-lit, an unopened bottle of bourbon in his hand. But like his wife, he kept his distance, offering a gruff hello.

Sean?

That boy was a story all on his own, gay but flirty as hell. Had Micah not warned him about my issues—which I knew he had—the guy would have been all up in my space. Within minutes, his carefree banter and smiles set me at ease.

While my age, he acted years younger, as though his maturity had gotten stuck in college. He'd been a frat boy and still behaved as one, exactly as Micah had warned me. Gay and proud, he bragged about his conquests, poking at Micah nonstop about opening an MM branch of elite for the entire two hours the three of them lingered in Micah's home.

My home.

I'd thoroughly accepted it as such with how we shared a bed every night and cooked together side by side whenever we weren't too lazy after a day spent in the office. He swore he didn't tire of me in those weeks. Didn't wish for a bit of space or silence even though I felt sure I sometimes intruded.

He would cling to me whenever time allowed, his face in my neck or hard cock in one of my holes. Well, not my ass —not yet. We discussed its eventual happening. But, baby steps.

We'd become masters at them, slowly, methodically expanding on how we loved on each other.

I also learned the reasons for his staunch integrity, the reason he kept his promises.

He hadn't heard from his old friend Dean in close to eighteen years, but the man had left a mark on Micah's life in a big way.

Micah had become the Dom he was because of that dark night on his eighteenth birthday. It was gruesome to hear, the words he shared cringeworthy. Sickening. Micah had been lucky to escape unscathed, even though Dean deserved to be locked behind bars for what he'd done.

Micah had learned his lesson, choosing to better his life, and I didn't judge him for what had been outside his control. I admitted to being thankful he'd come out of the assault that had taken place without it ruining his life.

I was also teary-eyed to find out he'd looked up Ginger a few years earlier. The woman had suffered from cancer at the time, and Micah had anonymously provided for all her needs, her bills, with her family none the wiser of the monetary donor who eventually covered funeral and burial expenses as well.

I'd told Micah he was a good man again that night—but I wasn't sure he'd believed me.

I watched as he interacted with his father. The man was negative to the deepest part of his marrow. Glass half-empty type, he had to point out possible awful scenarios on every topic even while the three men attempted to watch sports.

Micah's mom and I took care of the dishes, enjoying the quieter kitchen.

"I'm thrilled he's finally settling down," she said. "I've always worried about him..." she trailed off, rinsing the final pan from the dinner Micah and I had prepared for them thanks to Healthy Chef.

"He's the best man I've ever met," I stated with conviction, my heart full, the same as it had been since the night he'd reminded me of the power I held over my own destiny.

"It's surprising, really, considering how his father behaves." Micah's mom shook her head. "I put up with too much, but I vowed to honor and cherish." She drained the water from the sink and dried her hands. "Don't get me wrong—I love the man who gave my boys life, but sometimes I daydream about what might have been had I'd left him to his vices and demons."

I wasn't sure what to say to her openness. Build her up for her choosing loyalty and honoring her marriage vows? Offer her condolences for never having experienced the heart-fluttering love found in fairy tales?

I expected there would be bad times in the path ahead of Micah and I, but we'd agreed outside of actual vows before witnesses to hold each other's hands, to be there when the other needed. To offer support. Use kind words. *Listening* when the other spoke, not just hearing their voice.

Shit would happen, but he assured me every day of his feelings, his desire for me and my thoughts, that he wouldn't sway elsewhere.

I trusted him.

One hundred percent.

"I'm telling you, Micah—gay is the way to go!"

I bit my lower lip while walking behind Micah's mom into the living room. Sean was relentless to a fault, his voice loud and echoing through the downstairs.

"I don't want to have to deal with other size queens," Micah muttered. "You're a fucking handful, Sean—why would I willingly hire more like you to drive me insane?"

"Because you've landed yourself a pretty little sweetheart who will help soothe your grumpy pants at the drop of a hat." Sean's blue-eyed gaze shot to my face as I rounded the couch. "Tell him, Jasmine."

I held up a hand while perching on Micah's knee where he sprawled in his old recliner that had seriously seen better days. "I'm staying out of this one."

"Come on!" Sean whined. "You're his safe place. His peace."

Micah tugged me back against his chest and nuzzled my neck.

"Have you been talking about me again?" I asked, unable to help my smile or the happiness swelling inside my chest at Sean's declaration.

"Always." He pressed his lips beneath my ear, sending a shiver down my spine.

"Ugh—take it to the bedroom," Sean said, rolling his eyes. "Seriously. Some of us get turned off by that shit, you know."

"Yeah," Micah agreed. "I remember that feeling. But this one?" He squeezed me in his arms. "It's ten times better."

Sean snorted. "I'm just saying—"

"Enough, Sean." Their dad's barked order shut the younger son up. "Haven't you figured out yet that you don't always get your way?"

I glanced between the two men, slightly uncomfortable about their arguing.

"You're the one who spoiled me," Sean shot back, a smirk on his lips.

The man was full of piss and vinegar as my own dad would say.

"Only to shut your trap," the older Mr. Fox muttered.

"Who's playing?" his wife asked, an obvious attempt to redirect the conversation.

It was a Sunday afternoon football game—but I had no clue who faced who or if the season had even started yet. Sports played on the TV every weekend, but I never paid attention beyond Micah's warm body I snuggled against or the book I curled up with in our bedroom if his buddies gathered to watch the game together.

"Pats and Dolphins," Micah answered.

I settled against his chest, exhausted from the anxiety I'd dealt with leading up to our guests visit and lack of sleep the night before. Micah had woken me up during the early morning hours after claiming to watch me sleep. The creep had needed to feel how warm I was inside—his actual excuse for sinking into my body while I attempted to rouse myself from a dream where we'd been barefoot on the beach and holding hands.

My core warmed at the memory of how he'd loved on me gentle and slow, dragging out his enjoyment of being one with me. Caressing every inch of my body he could reach while holding me tight against him.

I would never get enough of his touch. His attention. His love.

The four-lettered word hadn't been directly spoken between us, but I felt it. I saw it too in his eyes whenever I caught him staring at me.

Somedays, we ended up fucking on his desk. Mine. In the office bathroom once. It no longer mattered that he was my boss and I was Elite's secretary. We belonged together.

"Little lamb." Micah's murmur against my ear roused me from a semi-dream state.

"Hmm?" I stretched, not realizing I'd been hovering on the edge of sleep.

He patted my thigh. "My parents are leaving."

"Sean driving them home?"

A chuckle rumbled his chest against my ear. "Yes, thank fuck."

I snickered and, blinking bleariness from my eyes, sat up.

Micah's mom helped his dad shuffle toward the front door. Sean stepped out of the half-bath to our right.

I climbed from my warm seat, hoping to curl back up the second they all left.

We exchanged goodbyes, his mom offering me a hug, which I stepped into and managed to handle without too much difficulty.

Sean came at me with open arms and a sly smirk on his lips.

Micah's slap to his chest halted the younger brother in his tracks. "Back off, asshole."

Sean did so, tossing me a wink. "Can't blame me for trying."

"You're a little shit," I muttered, grinning.

He blew me a kiss. "Love you too big sis."

"I'm only three months older than you."

"*Older* being the key word."

"Let's go, Sean," their mom said while leading their dad outside into the cooler summer evening. Her eye roll voiced loud and clear in her tone.

Micah and I stood on the stoop and watched them all pile into one car, Sean being their chauffeur as he'd been doing for a few years.

Micah released a groaned, heavy exhale as they drove away. "Thank fuck that's over."

"I think they're kind of sweet."

"You've *got* to be kidding me." He steered us back inside with his hands on my ass, bypassing the living room for the stairs.

I knew his plans. Could tell by the energy radiating off him.

"Sean has a point, you know," I stated casually, taking my time placing no-longer tired feet on the treads.

"Fuck," Micah muttered, slapping my ass to get me moving. "Not you too."

"Put him in charge of the gay branch."

"Are you shitting me?" He barked a laugh, hot on my slow heels as I made my way down the hallway toward our bedroom.

There was nothing better than stalling when Micah was in a rush to bury his dick inside me. Teasing tended to bring out his dominant side in the best ways possible.

I shrugged and stripped slowly, eyeing the bed. While I would have rather curled up together to nap, Micah gave off major vibes of needing a little loving in the wake of his father's negativity. He'd warned me about the moods he got into once his parents left.

"It might be good for Sean," I reasoned, being persistent with what I honestly thought might be exactly that. "Responsibility. Having to make decisions for someone other than himself."

"You really think that brat will grow up? You haven't known him nearly as long as I have."

I sprawled onto the bed, limbs out like a starfish, readying myself to be touched and smothered like Micah was fond of doing to me. "Maybe," I said, my thoughts trailing into oblivion as Micah stripped.

Damn, my man was fine as fuck. Those muscles, the virility that exuded off him in addictive waves.

I sighed, and he chuckled while climbing onto the mattress beside me rather than atop me. Rolling into him, I smirked. "What?"

"I love how you look at me," he said, drawing me close against his warmth. "Fuck—who am I kidding. I plain old love you, Jasmine. My little lamb." He tucked hair strands behind my ear as my eyes stung and heart ached over his admission. "Been wanting to tell you that for a while now, but I was afraid you would reason away my feelings and disagree."

"I won't ever dismiss your emotions," I promised with a whisper. "Same as you've never done with mine."

He rubbed his nose over mine in a tender motion, sighing a sweet exhale over my mouth.

"I love you too, Sir."

His arms tightened as he let out a groan exactly as I'd expected. "Goddamnit, woman," he growled. "I had every intention of spooning while you rested since I woke you up this morning, but then you gotta call me that." He shook his head.

I leaned in and nipped at his lower lip. "Show me how much you love me, Sir. Make me forget my name."

He obeyed my command without hesitation and thorough dedication.

Sleep came much later—for both of our exhausted bodies.

Chapter 25

Micah

"So where's this woman I've yet to meet?" Blake asked, sprawled out in the corner of my couch he'd claimed as his two years earlier when I'd held our first guy's sports day.

"You don't want to lay eyes on her," Reid tossed out before I could answer. "One wrong glance in her direction and Micah will knock your ass out like he did that Billy guy."

I rolled my eyes. "That fucker tried to do more than just look at her, dipshit."

"You should have put his nose through his skull," Cooney muttered.

"Got that right," Jarod agreed.

I glanced around my living room, loving the fact the five of us had freed ourselves for a Sunday afternoon of football. It had been months since we'd all managed to find a time when we were available to hang out.

Blake's Wren was at the pharmacy working. Jessie and Christine had taken both of Reid's kids to the park—brave souls—leaving him and Jarod with nothing to do. Like

Wren, Becky was on the clock. She'd recently been promoted to the weekend manager at the coffee shop she'd been working at, freeing the redheaded giant up for every get-together on Sunday afternoons.

And my woman all but Blake hadn't yet met? She was out running last-minute errands for Dina's wedding taking place the following Saturday.

"He gets out of jail and comes sniffing around ten years from now, and we're going to off his ass, bury him at sea while using your boat, Blake," Cooney said, letting out his darker side I enjoyed a little too much. Like me, he had zero tolerance for abusive men. He also knew how to bend morals when the situation called for...more important matters than doing the right thing in the eyes of society.

"Fuck yeah," Reid crowed, raising his hand like someone in a worship service. Nothing pleased him as much as seeing asshole exes behind bars.

My desires to hurt in order to bring pleasure used to bother me. Filled me with guilt. It had taken four years after that night with Dean before I had tried again to explore the kinks I couldn't get out of my mind. But that time, I'd done so in a safe environment with a seasoned Dom showing me what a D/s scene was really supposed to look like.

Years later, after submitting to his tutelage, I'd earned an invite to join Chantelle's club in downtown Boston where Cooney still frequented with his woman.

It had been months since I'd gone there.

While I hadn't mentioned visiting with Jasmine, I still held hope that someday she would be open to the idea of wearing my collar and calling me Master.

One step at a time.

"I bought Jasmine a ring," I stated, causing all four of my friend's heads to whip my way.

"No fucking way," Blake said, laughing. "The forever playboy—"

"You were the worst damn playboy, Harper," I shot back, cutting him off. "You could have any woman you wanted—so you did."

He preened a bit and huffed over his knuckles before rubbing them on his shirt.

Reid punched his shoulder. "Arrogant prick."

"No brag," he stated, his voice full of what Reid had accused him of. "Just fact."

"And Wren wrapped you up in a tidy little bow," Jarod said. "We know who wears the pants in your house."

"Becky is pregnant."

I jerked my head toward Cooney. "Get the fuck out!"

Other voices joined me as we congratulated Daniel until his face flushed.

"Finally got it up long enough to get the job done, huh?" Blake teased as I'd been about to do.

It was the pillow alongside Jarod that clobbered Blake upside the head for his comment. Reid's missed. "Don't be an ass," Jarod said.

Cooney chuckled, not taking offense. He'd never been a horny bastard like the rest of us until he'd met Becky. She was one of the sweetest submissives I'd ever met—aside from my own little lamb.

We still had a ways to go with the bucket list of deviant sexual acts she wanted to do with me we kept in the bedside table, but knowing she was willing made all the difference. It was her heart that mattered, not the anticipation of someday watching paddle prints bloom across her ass or filling her backdoor with a load of my spunk. That didn't mean I didn't hope for those things or tease her about them.

I loved her. Period.

In health or in sickness, the good times and the bad we would probably someday face. But, we would do so together. If she said yes to me, which Dina had assured me she would. Even her Dad and Mom had been on board when I'd asked their permission the week before when I'd taken them out to lunch without Jasmine knowing.

That outing had required a little white lie, but I reasoned it away, expecting Jasmine wouldn't mind once she learned why I'd snuck out to see them.

"I heard a rumor."

I glanced over at Jarod who rubbed at the beard he'd been growing in because Christine wanted him to.

We were all sickeningly wrapped around our women's pinkies. I couldn't find a single fuck to give over that fact. "What's that?" I asked Jarod.

"I was talking to Drake the other day at work—"

"Who's Drake?" Reid cut in.

"My shit head brother's best friend," I muttered. At least Drake acted his age and had a good head on his shoulders. If only he would rub off on Sean a little more.

"Drake told me that Sean said you're considering that MM branch for Elite he's been hounding you about."

I blew a slow exhale between my lips. "The fucker won't drop it."

A few of the guys had heard his whining that usually landed him whatever he wanted—but not from me.

"He needs an older guy to tie his ass up and spank him raw."

I snorted at Cooney's quiet declaration that was fucking. Spot. On. "Seriously. Maybe I should give in to him just to see if I can't find a Daddy looking for a sassy boy. I'd help to muzzle the little fucker myself. Might even take a belt to his ass and make him cry."

"Put him in charge," Blake suggested the same thing Jasmine had. "It's amazing what sudden responsibility will do to a man who shows no interest in growing up."

He knew firsthand about that shit. It had taken the early retirement of his father and the daily running of Harper's Construction that had settled him enough to start thinking about his future. Wren just happened to pop into his life at the right time, laying claim to his heart and tying his rich ass down without meaning or wanting to.

But she'd given in. Eventually.

"That's what Jasmine suggested," I said. "Make Sean the manager."

Blake grinned. "She must have a great mind—I like her already."

"Careful," Reid warned with a teasing smirk. "Old boss man is a little territorial."

He didn't lie, but I had nothing to worry about. Jasmine might allow her dad's touch, but the thought of any other guy getting up in her personal space still set her on edge and made inhaling difficult. Whatever it was about me, whatever connection we'd found, had bound us tightly together.

I just hoped like hell she felt the same way, that she would agree to be mine in every way until we both breathed our last.

Chapter 26

Jasmine

I stood on the other side of Liz, Dina's maid-of-honor, as my oldest sister and Aaron exchanged vows. Corseted into the navy bridesmaid dress and new heels pinching my toes, I fought boredom and a headache. Who knew weddings could be so damn stressful? And I wasn't even the one promising to honor, love, and cherish.

When Micah and I exchanged vows, it would be on the beach, and we would both be barefoot. Him in shorts, me in a breezy slip of a dress that allowed me to breathe the salt-scented air.

I tried for a decent-sized inhale and failed in the Catholic church's nave where we had grown up listening to priests drone on and on. While Liz had stayed true to the faith of our parents, I, along with Dina had gone our separate ways, but she still wanted to honor Mom by marrying in our childhood place of worship.

At least our parents still loved us after we'd chosen to leave their faith behind.

Aaron had been raised Baptist, and his parents were not happy he wasn't exchanging vows in *their* church. Scowls etched both their faces. I refrained from rolling my eyes and tried to pay attention to the priest speaking to my sister and her soon-to-be husband.

The back of my neck tingled, and I smiled. I'd noted where Micah sat when I'd walked down the aisle. Bride side, in the front row beside Liz's husband. Right where he belonged.

Warmth came to life between my thighs, and I squeezed them together at the thought of the night ahead. I'd readied an Elite bag two days prior and had hidden it beneath my side of our bed.

Micah and I had been discussing introducing some of my bucket list kink in the bedroom, and I felt ready to take another step. The thought of the nipple clamps I'd packed dampened my panties, and I bit the inside of my lip. The priest needed to hurry the fuck up.

Shifting on my feet didn't help. Allowing a sigh and straightening my shoulders in an attempt to stretch out didn't either. *Kiss the bride already*, I wanted to whine aloud.

The priest must have heard my thought, because a few seconds later, he encouraged Aaron to do so.

Fucking finally.

Turning and smiling along with the other five brides-maids as Dina and Aaron lip locked, I glanced over at Micah.

My breath caught. His blue-eyed gaze held mine, erasing the world and sounds of clapping hands. That erotic energy I missed whenever not with him zinged between us even though we didn't touch, weakening my knees.

I bit the inside of my lip as need for him swept through me, making me a little too warm regardless of the church's air-conditioning.

The bridesmaid to my right nudged my elbow.

I glanced around to find Liz had just descended the stairs and started back down the aisle.

Shit.

Two quick steps took me to the side of my escort, and I lightly touched my fingertips to the elbow he offered. Zero anxiety raised my blood pressure. Zero vise-effects strangled my chest. I kept my gaze on Micah until we passed his aisle and dropped my hand from my escort's arm the second we stood outside under the Indian summer sun.

I'd come a long way in the time I'd begun testing myself with Micah, but a receiving line...just, no. I slipped back into the church after a quick hug and kiss for Dina and a little wave for Aaron, hurrying to Micah's side as he waited near the front of the line behind my brother-in-law.

"You look amazing," he murmured in my ear, his hot breath causing goose bumps to break over my arms. "If you knew the thoughts I've been having since you walked down that aisle you would be a wet, panting mess with thighs spread and begging for my dick."

I shivered. If he was aware of my plans for the night ahead, he'd be hard and giving me the look that turned me so needy I begged.

Hanging on his arm, I ambled along with him as he congratulated and hugged first Aaron, then a beaming Dina.

"What the hell happened to my Mr. Grumpy Pants?" she asked, laughing and pulling away from him. "I've never seen you smile so much."

Micah squeezed me against his side and gazed down at me, his eyes full of emotion we had finally named aloud the week before.

"When's the wedding?" Dina asked with a snicker, but I shot my sister a glare, my cheeks flamed.

"Shut up," I muttered.

"Oh, please." She rolled her eyes. "Like you haven't gotten something all planned out in that brain of yours already, Jaz. Let me guess. Barefoot on the beach? Small and intimate with immediate family only?"

I snapped my suddenly unhinged jaw shut and tugged on Micah's arm, wanting the ground to swallow me whole.

"I'll have to get back to you on that, Dina," Micah said with a chuckle, hugging me again and allowing me to pull him farther down the receiving line, far from my runaway-mouthed big sister.

"Sorry about that," I muttered once we moved away from the lingering crowd outside of the church.

"I'm used to her unbridled tongue." He pulled me against him, and I rested my head against his chest. His heart beat strong in my ear, and I closed my eyes, soaking in his warmth.

Dina may have hit my fantasies spot on, but Micah and I took things one day at a time, testing waters, cultivating a richer relationship, and just plain old living life. I'd never been so happy.

Tonight, though, would be our—*my*—biggest test yet.

ℲⱢ

We escaped the reception as soon as possible without seeming rude, and although I'd danced most of the night away in Micah's arms like I'd wanted to do, the thought of what I planned made my insides tremble.

Micah had brought his cherry-red Ferrari, and we cruised home, windows down, the warm evening air tugging at my up-do that Liz had to pin since I couldn't relax enough for the hairdresser to do so. Micah's new fade that left the hair atop still long and sexily mussed up whipped around too. I stared at the beautiful man I'd been blessed with, as patient a soul as I'd ever met.

"What are you thinking?" he asked, squeezing my hand on the console.

"How lucky I am."

His smirk and quick, heated glance warmed me through. "I'm the lucky one."

He's a good one, I thought, rubbing my thumb along the back of his hand. And I planned on offering him myself in a way I didn't think he ever expected. Hoped for, yes, as he'd often admitted to.

We got home, and he poured us some wine before heading to the bedroom to rid ourselves of the restrictive clothing. He shrugged his suit coat off while I removed the opal jewelry Dina had gifted her bridesmaids.

"Can you help me with the bodice?" I asked, turning my back to him. I'd kept the ridiculous heels on and stepped out of the bunch of material that pooled at my feet a few seconds later, my breasts all but sighing in relief over the loss of the tight corset-type top.

Micah groaned and ran his hands down over my satin-covered ass cheek, nuzzling my neck. "I've been so hard for you all fucking day long."

I arched my back and wound my fingers into his hair as his hands slid up over my stomach to palm my breasts. He rolled and pinched my hard nipples, sending zings of need to my clit. My panties a soaking mess, I rubbed my ass against his upper thighs, and his cock jerked against my lower back.

"Are you wet for me?" he murmured over my ear.

"God, yes. Always."

He reached between my legs and cupped my pussy through my panties. "Take these off so I can see."

I stepped forward, my heartbeat pounding in my ears. Gaze on his face, I slipped my thumbs beneath the sides of my panties and pushed them down. I bent down to take them all the way off and continued sinking straight to my legs, kneeling in front of him, hands clasped and head bowed without being asked.

His sharp intake of breath filled me with the most intense joy that tears stung my eyes.

"Jasmine?"

"I'm yours—Master," I breathed the title he'd been craving even though he hadn't admitted to it. His eyes had told me, and I'd listened. Prepared myself in every way that I could. I trusted him for the rest.

A deep groan rumbled in his chest. "You're sure?"

"Yes." I lifted my head to peer up at the man who had changed my hopes for the future. The love of my life. "I want you, Micah. Every dark recess of your mind. If something proves to be too much, I promise to tell you to stop, and we can try again another day."

He straightened, his eyes emanating a look I'd never seen before, one of impassioned power and control.

Wetness oozed from my pussy to smear between my thighs, and I bit my lower lip as need shivered over my skin.

Without a word, he unbuttoned his slacks and pushed them to his knees, releasing his long, thick cock.

My mouth watered, and I licked my lips.

"Be a sweet little lamb and suck me."

A tremor rippled through me at his command that brooked no argument. I crawled forward and rose onto my knees before him. Pre-cum glistened at the tip as he held his cock out.

I lapped the saltiness from him and closed my mouth over the head, sliding down as far as I could.

He groaned and grasped my head with both hands. "Deeper." His voice rumbled as he nudged against the back of my throat.

I lifted my gaze and relaxed, allowing him to slide in like we'd been practicing.

"Just like that." His drawn-up balls tapped my chin. "Fuck, Jasmine, I'm inside your fucking throat. Goddamn."

He held me still and backed out, his silky heat caressing my tongue and lips, and I moaned my need. "I'm going to make you feel so good."

I whimpered, thinking for sure I would come without him even touching me. My breasts felt heavy, my nipples tight. Wetness smeared over my labia, and my clit ached. I rubbed my thighs together as he slid in to the hilt again, groaning.

"You like having my cock deep in your throat?"

"Mmm," I hummed my agreement, and he cursed again, pulling all the way out of my mouth.

"On the bed, minx," he said, kicking off his shoes and shoving down his pants.

I rose to totter in my heels with as much grace as my shaking body could muster, but rather than doing as he said, I rounded the footboard and pulled the goodie bag from beneath.

Another sharp inhale from him lifted my gaze as I returned to stand in front of him, black bag held out in offering.

His hand shook as he reached for it. "You disobeyed me," he murmured, unbuttoning his shirt with his free hand.

"I'm not sorry, Sir." I dropped my gaze, and he moved around me to the bed.

The sound of the bag's zipper opening sent a shiver down my spine.

"Hmm." Soft noises of his going through the contents echoed loudly in the quiet room.

I breathed in, counting to ten, focusing my mind to keep from begging for him to just touch me already.

"Come here."

I turned to find him sitting on the edge of the bed, nipple clamps in hand. Another rush of arousal coated my thighs.

He crooked a finger, and I closed the distance between us, stepping between his spread legs. His white dress shirt hung open, and I ran my gaze over his pecs, down his rippled abs, to the hard cock jutting up, its tip glistening again.

"Breathe, baby," he murmured and closed a clamp over my right nipple.

The sharp pain ripped through me, and I gasped as my clit tingled and pussy contracted. "G-God," I groaned, clenching my eyes shut.

"Okay?"

"Fuck yes," I didn't hesitate to answer truthfully. "S-So much better than your teeth."

"Mmm," he hummed his pleasure. "Enough pleasure to edge you?"

"Yes, Sir. *Definitely* yes."

He made another low, rumbling sound that curled through me like a stroke between my thighs. "No coming until I say so."

The other clamp closed over my left nipple, and I bit

down on my tongue to fight off the beginning of my climax tingling in my toes.

Pain did it for me. No fucking doubt about it. A couple other spankings—with him limiting his swings—had assured me of that truth, but I lusted for more. All of it.

"Don't hold back this time, Master," I whispered.

Micah groaned and pulled me down over his lap, my arms and breasts swinging free on one side, my heels reaching for the floor on the other.

His palm landed on my ass cheek without preamble, and I jolted with a stifled shriek.

Holy fucking shit that hurt like hell.

"Color?" he asked, his voice strained.

I wanted to see how much I could take before breaking. "Green, Sir."

Another landed on my other cheek, and I bit my lip to keep my cry contained. Two more landed lower than the first, and the stinging pain began to morph into a feeling I'd hovered on the edge of before but hadn't ever truly experienced. Tears ran down my cheeks, and my ears rang as he smacked the spot of the first swat. I groaned, arousal intense and throbbing in my core.

Micah reached between my thighs. "You're soaked." Satisfaction coated his voice thicker than the desire in my pussy. He pushed two fingers inside me, pulled them out, and slid them up my ass crack, smearing my slickness over my puckered hole.

"I think you need a little bling to go with these red cheeks," he murmured, and my thoughts ran to the jeweled plug I'd put in the bag.

Seconds later, a lubed, hard toy slid up through my soaked folds and rimmed my asshole. Micah teased me with its tip. I groaned as the plug eventually pressed against the tight ring of muscles protecting my virgin hole.

"Like that, Jasmine?" he asked, twisting the toy and probing a bit deeper.

Eyes clenched shut and panting for breath, I barely managed a whispered, "Yes." My toes began to tingle again, and I clenched my pussy, needing so much more.

Micah pushed the toy deeper, the slight sting of stretching disappearing the second he fully breached me, my muscle clenching around the smaller base.

An unexpected swat jolted me forward, swinging my breasts with their clamped nipples. "P-please..." I moaned.

"Please what?" Micah asked and landed another swat.

"Please put your dick in me, Sir."

He lifted and turned me, pulling me forward to straddle his lap on my knees, the fullness in my ass sending need pulsing through my entire body. Hand on his cock, he teased my pussy and tapped my aching clit.

I gasped and dug my fingers into the muscles on the tops of his tensed shoulders.

"No coming until I'm balls-deep inside of your pussy and give you permission," he said, tapping me again.

A low groan ripped through my chest as I fought off my climax.

He slid the head of his cock to my opening, and, hands on my hips, yanked me down, filling me with one thrust.

I shrieked as my climax ripped through me, my cum gushing around his hard length, my puckered hole clenching the plug shoved deep inside my ass.

Micah's firm grip held me still as I fought to squirm, gasping and begging him to fuck me. "Don't move," he growled and tugged on a nipple clamp with his teeth.

Another climax rolled over me at the sharp pain, and I shuddered in his arms.

"Naughty girl," he said, and I opened my eyes to find his heated gaze on my face. "I didn't give you permission to come," he murmured as my core continued to pull on the thickness filling me in euphoric spasms. "You disobeyed me twice now."

His gaze held pure control, the likes I'd never seen. Dominant and completely in charge.

Every inch of me melted as I gasped for breath, and I wanted to burrow inside him. Let him use me, give him pleasure. Anything he desired...

He lifted me by my hips and slowly lowered me onto his straining length again. "Your pussy is a perfect glove for my dick, Jasmine." A muscle jumped in his jaw as he groaned, and I squeezed my inner muscles around him, wanting him to lose his hold over his body until instinct made him fuck me with abandon.

He smacked my ass, and I moaned as my pussy clenched in response.

"Goddamn, baby," he growled and lifted me, only to slide in deep again. "You feel so fucking good."

I gyrated my hips, needing to rub my clit against him, but he tsked again and swatted. "I said not to move."

"Please, Micah," I whimpered.

"It's Master—or Sir—and you'd best remember that." He lifted me off his cock and turned me, hands palming my breasts and tugging the remaining clamp.

"Oh shit!" I squealed, my core pulsing.

"Middle of the bed," he ordered. "On your hands and knees."

After that first time of him taking me from behind, something had clicked into place. I no longer needed him to talk to me nonstop while loving on me in that position. Awareness of him remained in the forefront of my mind. Wetness coated my thighs clear to my knees, but all I cared about was Sir shoving his cock back inside me and fucking me until I passed the fuck out.

My muscles shook, but I kicked off my heels and climbed onto the bed, expecting the stinging lash of the flogger I'd put in the bag.

"So beautiful," Micah said as the mattress dipped behind me. His hands smoothed over my heated backside. "Gorgeous." He tapped the jewel on the butt plug, and I moaned, pressing back toward him.

"I need to have you here," he murmured, tapping again, "and I'm guessing since you put a massive bottle of lube in this bag for such a tiny plug that you're hoping for the same."

"Yes, Sir. I'd like to try."

I gasped as he fucked me a few times with the toy, teasing my rim on its widest part. "Sir," I whined.

Micah pulled the plug out, leaving me empty and panting. The snap of the lube cap heightened my pulse.

Cool wetness dribbled over my puckered hole, and I lowered my head to the mattress, licking my dry lips, my heartbeat a fluttering mess as he used first one finger than a second to encourage my hole to stretch even further. He spread me open with his thumbs. "Fuck, minx...I can see the pink walls inside your ass. Looks so smooth and hot. Can't wait to push my dick inside you."

"Jesus, Sir." I croaked, then hissed as he worked in a third finger.

"Color?"

"Green—but that burns a bit."

"Mmm." He didn't stop but continued to slowly fuck in and out of my body, loosening my hole for his girth.

A swat sounded in my ears before I registered any pain.

Low groaning escaped my lungs, and I writhed back against his fingers. "More—please, Sir."

"Fuck, I love it when you beg me like that." Micah slid free of my ass, leaving me so damn empty I wanted to cry.

Seconds later, his slick cock slid up through my cheeks as he squeezed and kneaded my burning flesh. "I'll make it good for you, baby. I promise."

I exhaled on a deep sigh and tried to relax. "I trust you."

The blunt tip of his cock pressed against me, and I bore down, knowing it would make things easier.

His thick head stretched my muscle ring, setting my ass on fire before he even breached me.

"Oh, God!" I gasped.

"Color, baby?" he groaned, his voice breaking.

"G-Green. I-I think." I licked my lips. "Green."

He grasped my hips and slowly pushed forward until he slid past my tight muscle.

"Fuck!" I cried out and gulped, the pain too much. "Holy shit, Sir." I whimpered, and he held still, barely inside my ass.

"Too much?" he rasped, hands soothing over my burning cheeks.

I hissed, panting. "N-No. Just...wait. I-I need a second. I can do this."

"I know you can, little lamb. You're so fucking brave. Strong."

His words sent an ache through my chest, and even though I considered using my safeword to stop the pain in my ass, I wanted to gift him use of my body.

"The worst is over, baby," he crooned, sliding his hands

up my sides and down my back. "Promise it'll be better from here on in."

Out, I almost argued. "M'kay—give me more," I chose to say instead.

I bore down, and Micah pushed in what felt like a goddamn foot, simply making me feel full rather than intensifying the burn.

"Holy shit, you're huge," I choked on a shaky laugh.

"Not sorry," he stated as though through gritted teeth, his voice nothing but lust and love.

Micah's cock stretched me beyond what I'd thought possible. He continued to work his way inside me in slow increments, and I struggled to breathe when he finally bottomed out, his balls kissing my sopping pussy.

"Christ, Jasmine." He backed out so fucking slowly I wanted to scream at him for teasing me, but he pushed in fully, making me want to holler for an entirely different reason. Who knew getting fucked up the ass would be the most exquisite pain/pleasure feeling on the face of the earth?

Mine, at least.

"Your ass is so fucking tight. God*damn*, baby." Another slow glide out and in, and I dropped my chest to the mattress, my clamped nipple rubbing at the sheet and sending rippling zings straight to my clit.

"Oh shit," I groaned, clenching my ass around his cock that no longer battled for entry into my relaxed hole.

He hissed, held still while buried deep, and swatted my ass cheek.

"Fuck!" I shrieked, jerking forward slightly, but the sting didn't lessen my arousal. I pushed back to impale myself again.

"Mmm," he hummed his approval, and I shifted toward

the headboard again, loving the slick drag of his thickness through my muscle ring.

He swatted the other cheek.

"M-Master," I groaned. "Sir..." I worked myself back and forth on his dick, every inch of my skin going tight.

He landed two more blows on my backside, harsher than the first, and I trembled, desire coursing through me. Buzzing my brain. Rushing my pulse to thump in my ears.

"*Please*, Sir," I moaned, deeply arching my back to better fuck myself on his length.

"Do you need to come?" he asked, grasping my hips to hold me still.

I whimpered, trying to wiggle in his hold. "God, yes. Need it so fucking bad."

He reached a hand around my hip and coated his fingers in my wetness, his dick attempting to buck deep inside my ass. "Christ, Jasmine. Your body loves my cock."

I grunted an agreement, trying again to fuck myself on him.

His slickened fingers rubbed over my clit, and I bit my lip, trying like hell to wait for his permission that time.

The warmth and hardness of his chest pressed against my back as he pulled out to the tip. "Come for me, baby." He pinched my clit and slammed into me, sliding my chest and clamped nipple across the mattress.

I screamed as my climax exploded through my body.

"Fuck," Micah growled and grasped my hips in a bruising grip, slamming into my ass over and over as I shuddered and groaned my drawn-out climax. "I'm going to fill your ass with my cum." He lay over my back as I slumped to the mattress, his breath hot on my ear.

I managed a groan, trying to lift my ass as he continued to thrust me against the bed.

"You're mine, Jasmine."

"Yes!"

"Every fucking inch of you."

"God, yes!"

Another climax ripped through me, making my brain spin.

"Fuck yes!" Micah shouted. "Goddamn, baby." His cock jerked deep in my ass, and I swore I felt the heat of his cum deep inside of me as he growled and shuddered against my back.

I lay like a rag doll beneath his weight, tingles of complete satiation sweeping through my body.

Micah kissed my shoulder, my neck, his hot breath caressing my ear. "I love you so fucking much it hurts."

Tears stung my eyes, and he brushed my hair off my cheek, his lips trailing to my lips. I turned my head, and he captured my mouth with a groan.

"So fucking much," he murmured over my lips.

A sob caught in my throat, and he pulled out, his cock sliding free from my ass and leaving me uncomfortably empty.

"Hey." He gently turned me onto my back and the heat from my probably reddened ass cheeks brought a gasp to my lips. "You okay?"

I grabbed his arms and pulled him down on top of me, needing his warmth. His touch all over me. I wound my fingers into the silky strands of his hair. His sated blue eyes stared into mine, full of concern and so much emotion that my chest ached.

"I love you too," I whispered. "There's nothing I wouldn't do for you, Sir—nothing."

His smirk eased the hurt in my chest, flooding me with happiness I'd never thought existed. "So what about meeting me barefoot on the beach to repeat our own vows?"

I released a slow exhale, taking back that curse I'd rained down on my sister's head. "A thousand times, yes."

Micah half-rolled off the bed, grabbed his slacks, fishing for something from the pocket. He returned, brushed his lips across mine, gentle yet searing. "Next week?" he murmured, zero trace of teasing in his voice as he slid an engagement ring onto my left hand.

A tear slipped down my cheek as I nodded, unable to speak or chide him for the ridiculous size of the diamond.

"I'll promise to honor and cherish you the rest of my life, Jasmine," he stated with conviction, his dark blue eyes swelled with love and wetness.

I smiled through my tears and leaned up to kiss him, knowing I could trust my Sir.

Epilogue

Jasmine

It ended up being two weeks to the day that I met Micah on the beach as he'd asked of me. A borderline cool breeze blew in off the ocean, rippling my hair I'd left down to flow as free as the white sundress I wore for my wedding day. No shoes or sandals protected my feet from the sand.

Micah's welled eyes studied me as Dad and I drew nearer where he stood with a Justice of the Peace, my mom, his parents, Sean and a plus-one, and Liz's family. Dina was in Europe somewhere on her own honeymoon, but I hadn't been about to wait an entire month for her to get home for me to take Fox as my last name until death parted Micah and I.

He'd put a ring on my finger, and I'd refused to give him time to back out. Not that he would. The man was smitten with me, same as I was with him, and we couldn't wait. Didn't want to.

Sure, we'd married quickly, but what about our whirl-wind romance hadn't been fast?

When you knew, you knew. Why waste time and put off starting our forever we both desperately wanted?

Sean's flavor of the month sighed as I hurried past the two men. I couldn't imagine Ron—or was it Rob?—would last very long. He was too much of a pushover. Micah's little brother needed someone with a stern hand, a man who could say no to him.

But those thoughts could definitely wait.

The love of my life smiled at me as though I lit his world like the sun every morning shining over our bed through blinds he left open. Surprisingly, with his warmth beside me while falling to sleep, I rarely needed a night-light.

"Damn, Jasmine," he murmured when I finally stood in front of him.

Dad handed me over, and I clasped both of Micah's hands in mine with a death grip. Nerves fluttered my belly, but I'd never been more sure of anything in my life. We exchanged our vows while barefoot on the beach, fulfilling one of my dreams. I hoped to do the same with dozens more in the coming years.

The man officiating declared us husband and wife, and Micah swept me up into his arms, spinning me around, our mouths fused together. Liz had captured a picturesque image of us in that moment, sunshine glinting in my hair, a hazy-white aura around us, cradling us both as though the rays wrapped us in love.

I grew teary-eyed over the image she showed me on her phone once we celebrated in the basement of that Italian restaurant where Micah and I had gone for our official first date. I'd put on sandals and wore a sweater since the Indian summer's sunshine couldn't keep us warm.

We rented out the entire basement area but didn't bother with any music beyond the Italian opera seeping from hidden speakers. At least there was a small bar area in the corner with someone manning the station for those of us who drank.

Liz's older son ripped around the room, giggling as his daddy chased him. My conservative parents held glasses of water while Micah's mom sipped on white wine. His dad held a tumbler half-filled with ice and amber liquid. He would end up in an early grave, but that was what happened when stubbornness ruled rather than better sense. At least Micah knew when to bend a bit.

His greatest act of loosening his hold on control had been in giving up trying to stifle his desire for me. He'd made a good choice, as had Dina, in gifting me her job.

I owed her one.

Maybe I would name my firstborn after her if we ever decided to have kids. That wasn't something near the top of our to-do list. We wanted to enjoy each other without the added stress of responsibility for another little human for a few years. Neither of us cared either way if we produced a vomit and shit factory anytime soon.

But to eventually hold a tiny, smitten image of my love and smother it with affection?

I hadn't hesitated to jot that item down under *someday*.

Sipping my wine, I studied my husband—God, I adored that word—as Sean got all up in his space, lips moving as always. I snickered and shook my head. Micah needed to just give in already.

"Never thought I'd see the day, Jaz," Liz stated quietly.

I turned to find her studying me as she rocked side-to-side with my sleeping nephew. I set aside my wine and held out my hands.

"Nuh uh." She shook her head, turning to the side to keep him from my grasp. "The little nugget is sleeping and letting me snuggle. You can have him when he wakes up, wails, and attempts to beat my boobs into submission."

I held in my snort. She had no clue about Micah's and my lifestyle. No way would she understand or approve either.

The baby had been crying right before Dad had led me onto the beach but had thankfully quieted when Liz had shoved said boob in his face—I'd found out later. I'd just been thankful for the peace as Micah and I had exchanged our vows.

To love, honor, and cherish...we'd done away with the whole obey thing. No one but the two of us needed to know about our dynamic in the bedroom—and the new playroom Micah had begun putting together in the guest room adjacent to ours. He'd had Blake's company come in and cut a door in between the two rooms, making use of our master bathroom and bed for aftercare more convenient.

He'd also brought up the idea of visiting Chantelle's, a club for all things kink. Since the GIFs and old porn I'd seen when studying the lifestyle had turned me on, I'd agreed. Besides, he had a membership going to waste.

I'd added a date night at the club to my bucket list in the bedside table without his knowing, and I couldn't wait for him to see it.

"So how are we going to celebrate?" Micah whispered against my ear after finally escaping his little brother.

"Flogger," I tossed out and sipped my wine without looking at him.

He didn't speak, and I glanced over to find him staring at me with that heated gaze that did funny things to my insides.

"I love it when you look at me like that," I whispered.

His eyes darkened. "How's that?"

Our conversation sounded too familiar, and I smiled, toying with the top button of his white linen shirt. "Like you want to tie me to the four posters of our bed and lay stripes along my back."

Micah legit growled under his breath. "You can't say shit like that when we're in public."

I patted his chest and winked. "Think about whatever Sean was just filling your ears with. I'm sure it'll help keep your dick deflated for a while longer."

"Little lamb..." Micah warned, and I snickered, sashaying away.

He loved it when I got sassy—especially since he now could punish me in ways that brought serious pleasure that drained us both.

I expected the flogger to be similar to a spanking.

I'd never been more wrong.

Thin leather straps—lots of them—licked at my skin two hours later after Micah had stripped me of my wedding dress and tied me to our bed like I'd suggested. The flogger stung but with more heat than jolting pain.

Warmth spread over my back and thighs, and I sank into the feel, seeing each lash as an extension of my Sir's loving hands. Arousal had already slickened between my thighs before we'd begun the scene, and my need only intensified with every strike.

My brain buzzed, my nerve endings alive and full of static. Even though haziness crept into the corners of my mind, I felt as though I walked the edge of combustion. My breaths weren't quickened but deep and calm. Thoughts quieted into numbness.

Hands caressed over my spine...my shoulders. Back down to the tops of my heated ass cheeks.

I sighed, turning my head.

"Okay, little lamb?" Micah asked quietly, still touching me, bringing me slowly back from wherever I'd gone.

"I-I feel fucking *amazing*," I moaned, and he chuckled. "Make love to me, husband."

"Let me untie you first."

"No—just like this," I muttered, my voice muffled from laziness.

Micah kissed my forehead before leaving my line of sight.

I shut my eyes again and just felt.

His hands on my splayed thighs. His fingers between them, checking how aroused I was to take his thick cock.

"You liked my flogger, didn't you, baby?"

"Mmm," I moaned my agreement, my hips moving a bit on instinct.

"Need my dick?"

"Yes," I whispered, lifting my hips toward his teasing fingertips.

He chuckled again, but I didn't have the energy to get mouthy with him for denying me what I wanted.

Micah planked over me, his hard length pressing against my ass crack. He nosed over my hair, pressing soft kisses to the back of my head. "Love you, my sweet wife." Shifting his hips, he notched his cock into my pussy and glided forward.

I hissed at the feel of his pelvis moving over my lashed backside—but it felt good. Addictively so.

He lowered his body and fucked into me with slow gyrations, like some dirty dance music played, thumping through our blood. I moved against him in perfect rhythm, once more skirting that edge of floating as his muscles and skin shifted over my hot skin.

"Love you," I finally murmured a reply, clutching at the sheets beneath my bound fists.

"Want you to cream all over my balls," Micah whispered against my ear while sliding his hands beneath my body. He cradled my chest with one arm, the other hand snaking down between my thighs. "Mmm," he moaned while trailing his fingers over where he thrust into me with slow strokes. "So wet for me. This pussy loves my dick, doesn't it?"

"Yes, Sir," I moaned as he flicked over my clit with too soft of a touch.

"Want me to make it hurt?"

"Mmm," I moaned an agreement, my mind once more buzzing.

Micah tugged on my throbbing nub, but not enough to send me tumbling into euphoric bliss.

"More," I begged and licked my dry lips. "Need it."

Micah nuzzled my cheek, my neck. "Come for me, little lamb." He pulled on my flesh—and twisted.

I bucked beneath him, crying out his name, gasping out my love—curses and sobs as I came around his thrusting cock.

"That's it. Milk me, baby. Make me cum and fill you up." He grunted. Shuddered. Wet heat spilled deep inside me as he squeezed me tight. "Fuck, Jasmine. Jesus, you're so good." A gulp sounded loud in my ear, but whatever noises he made while emptying inside me faded as I slid into the place I never expected to find.

Peaceful perfection beneath the care of my Sir. My husband.

Bonus Epilogue

Micah

It was almost midnight on the Saturday night between Christmas and New Year's Eve, and everyone was stirring in the ballroom—every little mouse.

I huffed at the Dicken's story flitting through my brain while looking out over the crowd of people we had invited to the Elite Escort's holiday party. Between current employees, their plus ones, past escorts and their families, and mine as well as Jasmine's, we numbered close to one hundred people.

Pride swelled my chest, and I couldn't keep from grinning.

Everyone had dressed to the nines, sequins and jewels glittering in the lights. But Jasmine outshone them all. Diamonds encrusted the collar/choker I'd gifted to her on Christmas morning, and it had been the sole thing on her body when I'd made love to her afterward beneath our tree glittering with lights and garish tinsel she'd insisted on hanging from every bough.

Anything for my love.

She glanced at me from where she stood talking to her

parents. Warmth filled me as she toyed with the necklace I'd given her as a symbol of ownership to anyone aware of the BDSM lifestyle. Pink flushed her cheeks as though she recalled what I'd done in that moment. The sharing, the warmth between two souls entwined beyond what I'd ever hoped for.

Jasmine had started out as my secretary and had become my entire world.

Everyone else in that room, all of Elite, could dissolve into nothing but memories, and I wouldn't care as long as she continued to hold my hand.

Her parents didn't have a clue as to the meaning behind my gift draped around her graceful neck, but they had been informed about what I did for business. It had been an uncomfortable few weeks after I sat them down and filled them in on why I was able to spoil their youngest daughter in the way I did, but things had seemed to smooth over.

They'd shown up for the company party, something I'd felt sure they wouldn't do.

Perhaps befriending my parents shortly after our wedding had helped. Neither my mother nor my father held alcohol in their hands, but water and a soft drink like my in-laws. The four had become close, meeting up to play cards almost weekly.

With no booze in or allowed in the Swift's home, my father had started giving up the bottle that one night a week. After Thanksgiving with both blended families packing out my and Jasmine's home, he announced he was done with alcohol for good.

Sean, however, hadn't changed one goddamned bit. His latest flavor of the month wouldn't last any longer than the previous three since Jasmine and I had exchanged vows on the beach, barefoot like Dina had predicted. But I had a plan—I was about to gift him his Christmas present.

But, I did so out of pure selfishness.

One, to shut him up.

Two, to make Elite even more money.

I'd done some research and had quietly tested the market on the side with only a few people in the know. We were going to give EEMM a try—with Sean at the helm. But I would stand behind him. Direct him if necessary and definitely clean up whatever messes he made until he settled into his role of responsibility that I hoped would help him grow the fuck up.

"Ready to begin the headache of a lifetime?"

I'd been so wrapped up in my thoughts I hadn't realized Blake had sidled up to me. Clinking my glass of wine against his bottle of beer, I smiled. "You and Jasmine had better be right about this idea ridding myself of the biggest pain in my ass."

"It's going to work. That guy you hired last month..." He paused, allowing me to fill in the blank.

"Kellen."

"Yeah—he's living proof this gay branch is going to explode. Might even eventually take over the straight escort side of the business."

I doubted it, but Kellen had been the turning point for me.

We'd been friends back in college, but while I'd been all about the ladies, he hadn't cared what was in a person's pants. He was attracted to people, period. Pussy, dick, it didn't matter, although he tended to date more guys than women and loved bottoming as much as he did topping other men.

While we hadn't kept in touch a whole lot over the

years, I knew he'd moved back to the Boston area. I'd reached out to him to see if his love of sex and aversion to monogamy still dictated his nightlife. He'd told me those stances had more than doubled after a serious heartbreak a few weeks earlier.

So I'd made him an offer he couldn't refuse.

He stood with Sean and Drake—I hoped Sean's gay best friend would be on board for what I had planned too. The guy was beefy and I could admit good-looking with his dark hair and blue eyes. He was the opposite of my brother at least. Large and quiet. Two qualities I knew I would appreciate more than Sean's loud, leaner type if I were into guys.

"When are you going to drop the bomb?" Blake asked, and I sipped my wine, eyeing my brother.

He'd already had too much to drink as was usual. The boy loved his beer. At least he hadn't gotten into the hard stuff like our father and could go dry for weeks at a time when he stubbornly declared he could just to prove it to me.

Kellen caught my eye, and I motioned him over with my head.

He spoke to Sean for a few more seconds, clasped his shoulder, and made his way toward me. Sean wasn't aware Kellen had been taking on male clients for the past two months, and I'd asked my newest hire to keep the truth from him until I'd made my announcement.

Didn't want to ruin the surprise.

"Ready?" he asked with a grin, his hazel-green eyes a bit hazed over from whatever he'd been drinking.

"Ready." I got the DJ's attention, and he wound down the music. Taking his mic, I turned to face the crowd. "Good evening friends and family of Elite!" I said, quieting everyone except for those who'd had a bit too much to drink

—like Sean who whooped his delight to be partying with us all.

"I hope you're having a great time," I continued, and a few more catcalls and hollers sounded around the ballroom. "For those currently on my payroll—you're welcome. Make sure you spend those bonuses wisely. For those who left me because you went and fell in love—your loss!"

I raised my wine as laughter broke out. "Just kidding. You—*we* gained something more precious than diamonds."

I glanced over at my wife who beamed at me, her cheeks flushed.

"I wanted to take a minute to thank you all for all your hard work." More titters broke out unsurprisingly, hearing my intended pun. "For your dedication and loyalty to Elite. You've made me a shit ton of money, I won't lie, but I've also gained countless friends I value more than the almighty dollar. I was thinking earlier tonight that this business we've built together —" I swept my hand over the crowd "—could disappear from existence, and the most important thing would still remain. Love. For our women, for our families—sisters. Brothers."

I met Sean's gaze. He grinned like a dork and lifted his bottle of beer.

"Sean."

"Yeah, big bro?" he hollered.

I pulled a business card out of my back pocket and held it out toward him.

Drake elbowed him, and my brother sheepishly strode forward. At least he didn't stumble or weave—so he wasn't drunk off his ass, thank fuck.

"Merry Christmas," I said as he took the card, and I rubbed his hair in the way that had always earned me a punch when he'd been younger.

He stared at his name in gold lettering. "No. Fucking. Way!" His voice rose with every word, and he jerked his head up, his smile wide, and blue eyes similar to my own lit the fuck up.

I turned my focus on the crowd, scanning over faces of people I would die for. Kill for. Quite a few closer to my heart than my own blood. "I'd like to make the official announcement that Elite Escorts has created a gay branch— and Sean Fox will be acting as the manager."

He let out another whoop and actually did a little dance.

People broke out into applause, but there was more laughter than anything else.

"It's about fucking time!" Someone yelled from a corner of the room.

"I'm hiring!" I called back to whoever was on board with my plans for expansion.

Sean threw his arms around me, squeezing me tight, and I lowered the mic to hug him one-armed. "Thanks, Micah." It sounded as though tears clogged his throat. "I'm not going to let you down."

"I know you won't. This opportunity is going to give you a reason to find more in life than partying all the time, and you're going to make us both wealthy as fuck."

"Can I whore myself out too?" he asked, pulling away and laughing although wetness hazed his eyes.

I snorted. "As if I would expect you to sit in an office rather than bend over as part of your new job."

"You're the best." He grabbed my face and planted a kiss on my lips.

"Ugh, seriously?" I wiped over my mouth as he turned toward my wife.

"Sorry!" He laughed his apology at Jasmine and headed for Drake.

Little fucker. He was going to drive me nuts. Maybe I would get him an office separate from the one attached to my home. I would definitely need another secretary to help my wife handle the workload since she'd picked up Tuesdays in the office once we'd secretly expanded.

"Bar's open!" I spoke into the mic, my voice easily heard over the guests who'd begun to talk amongst themselves again. "Happy holidays—and get an Uber if you've had more than one drink!"

People lifted said drinks, and we all pretended to clink our glasses and bottles together. The guests went back to party mode.

Blake clasped my shoulder and disappeared into the crowd, murmuring something about finding his little birdie.

Jasmine met me halfway as we both strode toward one another to lessen the distance between us. "He seemed happy."

I snorted a laugh. "You think?" I wrapped my arms around my wife's waist and held her close. "New year is coming up soon. Any resolutions?"

She shrugged. "Not really. Just plans."

"Such as?"

"Crossing off a few more of those deviant items on my bucket list."

"Oh?" I asked, curious to what she wanted to try out first.

Jasmine toyed with my tie and smoothed down my starched lapels that didn't need straightening. "Well, since we crossed off the crop and paddle—which I loved both if you remember."

I did. Vividly enough that my dick twitched at the

memory of the marks I'd left on her skin, how she'd flown into subspace even before climaxing.

"So I was thinking...remember that final gift I told you to keep beneath the tree?"

"Yeah." I wondered what she'd had planned.

"I had every intention of giving it to you Christmas morning, but then you handed me this." She ran her fingertips over the choker around her smooth neck. "And I decided to wait a bit longer."

"Are you going to tell me what's in that box, or do I need to guess?" I asked when she didn't expand.

Her pupils began to swell as pink darkened her cheeks.

I knew the length and width of the package. Had seen similar boxes plenty of times. The sight of it under the tree a few days earlier had spiked lust through my blood—until she'd told me to leave it for later.

Leaning in close, I exhaled over her ear, loving how she shivered in my arms. "A cane."

Jasmine jerked back and slapped my shoulder. "You peeked!"

"I did not!" I laughed.

She pouted, and I planted a quick kiss on her lips.

"I didn't," I insisted, keeping right up in her face. "I'm intuitive, remember? I could tell you were nervous about giving it to me, that it was something big—emotionally. It's the toy that scares you the most. The one I've mastered because of my past."

My wife swallowed and nodded, fiddling with my tie. "Next year. I want to try next year."

"Are you thinking January first or the next holiday season?"

She snickered but once more gave me her pale-eyed

gaze I still wanted to drown myself in. "How about February sixteenth?"

"Your birthday."

"Yes."

"That sounds more like a happy birthday to me though."

Jasmine wrapped her arms around my neck, pushing up onto her toes to get closer to me. "Haven't you figured out yet that gifting you every inch of my body is what brings me the most satisfaction and joy in life?"

I pressed my mouth to hers, barely withholding from slipping my tongue between her soft lips. Groaning, I pulled back since it would be hours before I could strip her down and make her come on my cock. "You're the best thing to happen to me, little lamb."

She tucked her face against my chest with a sigh. "And your beating heart is the one I will trust through this life and hopefully our next."

My eyes stung, and I lowered my head and kissed the top of hers. She smelled of flowers and springtime. Life and love.

Mine.

THE END

About the Author

USA Today bestselling author Lynn Burke is a CrossFit and coffee addict. Her three spawn dictate how often she can be found hunched over her Mac, typing as fast as her fickle muse cooks up hot stories.

You can find more about Lynn at her website: www. authorlynnburke.com

Also By Lynn Burke

Abel's Obsession

Divulging Secrets

Healing Storms

In Between

Reluctant Lumberjack

Resisting his Mate

Billion Dollar Love Anthology

Blood Born Series

Bonds of Worship Series

Dark Leopards MC

Darkest Desires Series

Devil's Outlaws MC

Elite Escort Series

Elite Escorts MM Series

Fallen Gliders MC

Forbidden Obsession Duet

Found by Fate Series

Midnight Sun Series

Missing Link Series

Risso Family Series

Sandy Ridge Series

Sinful Nature Series

Vicious Vipers MC

Vicious Vipers MC

www.ingramcontent.com/pod-product-compliance
Lightning Source LLC
Chambersburg PA
CBHW070455200726

48293CB00007B/2205